WAVING AT THE GARDENER

WAVING AT THE GARDENER

The Asham Award Short-Story Collection

Edited by Kate Pullinger

Foreword by Liz Calder

BLOOMSBURY

LONDON · BERLIN · NEW YORK

First published in Great Britain 2009

Selection copyright © The Asham Trust 2009
Foreword copyright © Liz Calder 2009

The copyright of the individual stories remains
with the respective authors.

'Rape Fantasies' by Margaret Atwood is from *Dancing
Girls and Other Stories* © 1977, published by McClelland
and Stewart. Reprinted with permission of the author.

The moral right of the authors has been asserted

Bloomsbury Publishing, London, Berlin and New York

36 Soho Square, London W1D 3QY

A CIP catalogue record for this book is
available from the British Library

ISBN 978 0 7475 9876 3
10 9 8 7 6 5 4 3 2 1

Typeset by Hewer Text UK Ltd, Edinburgh
Printed in Great Britain by Clays Ltd, St Ives plc

Mixed Sources
Product group from well-managed
forests and other controlled sources
www.fsc.org Cert no. SGS-COC-2061
© 1996 Forest Stewardship Council
FSC

www.bloomsbury.com/ashamaward

www.ashamaward.com

CONTENTS

LIZ CALDER

Foreword

A short story *occurs*, in the imaginative sense. To write
one is to express ... the life-giving drop – sweat, tear,
semen, saliva – that will spread an intensity on the page;
burn a hole in it.

Nadine Gordimer

FROM THE point of view of the reader, the prospect
of opening a new collection of short stories is more
challenging than embarking on a novel, because each new
story demands a new commitment. With this is mind, I can
assure prospective readers that *Waving at the Gardener* offers
a feast of 'life-giving drops'. The acid test comes at starting
the next story: eagerly or with sinking heart? And has the
intensity of the last story burned a hole in one's memory? Can
we remember it an hour, a week or a year after reading it?

Selected from more than 800 entries, these twelve stories,
plus four commissioned from established writers, making
up this heart-lifting assembly, will undoubtedly keep the
reader engaged from start to finish. And they will linger
long in the memory.

While their territories stretch across the globe, from
frozen lakes in Canada to the war zones of Palestine,
low-rent Glasgow and the Malayan jungles of the 1960s,
these stories are bound together by universal themes: the

struggle for survival, the search for love, family traumas, the shadow of death and the hope of rebirth.

What is very striking in this collection is the similarity of cause and effect in story after story, whether it is in 'Omi's Ghosts', Alison Dunn's powerfully moving story of two friends violently torn apart by the Jamaican gun culture they grow up in, or the young racist thugs succumbing to violence and gang warfare on the streets of London in Catherine Chanter's 'A Summary of Findings'. Broken homes, failed dreams, sexual hopes and family loss pervade many of these gritty tales, as in the terrifying opening story, 'The Thaw' by Alison MacLeod. Mothers and daughters, mothers and sons, fathers and daughters, best friends, sisters, all these everyday relationships give rise to eternal dramas. The title story, 'Waving at the Gardener' by Liz Day, is a painfully touching monologue by a woman who has had a stroke but finds a late-flowering sexual joy in fancying a virile young gardener, while her coldly uncaring husband wishes she were out of his hair (such as there is). Together these stories make a brilliant multifaceted portrait of the times we live in and present a tremendously heartening display of talent and artistry.

While the short story battles for recognition and prestige among the higher profiles of novels, plays and poetry, writers struggle to find outlets for their work, making such initiatives as the Asham project crucial to its survival. The high standards of past and present Asham Collections are clear evidence of a hugely fertile generation of new writers. Bloomsbury is very proud to have been associated with the publication of these sparkling anthologies and to have witnessed so many promising debuts.

What ultimately matters with short stories, as with all fiction, is that the 'voice' arrests and convinces, and that the stories move, disturb and grip the reader. What is important to the prospective writer is encouragement and the right channels to aim for, which is why the Asham Collection is so vital.

Liz Calder
Co-founder, Bloomsbury Publishing

- *If you love short stories, look out for the short story festival –* **Small Wonder** *– organised jointly by the Asham and Charleston Trusts, which takes place at Charleston near Lewes, East Sussex, every September.*
- *For more information about this and other literature projects, visit www.ashamaward.com or www. charleston.org.uk.*

THE ASHAM AWARD WINNERS 2009

First prize   Jo Lloyd for 'Because It Is Running By'

Second prize   Hilary Plews for 'Lily's Army'

Third prize   Cherise Saywell for 'The Candle Garden'

The judges for the Asham Award 2009 are Di Speirs, executive producer for BBC Radio 4; Erica Wagner, novelist, short story writer and literary editor of *The Times*; and David Constantine, short story writer, novelist, poet and translator.

The Asham Award is supported by
Much Ado Books of Alfriston, East Sussex;
the John S. Cohen Foundation
and Rees Elliott of Lewes.

ALISON MACLEOD

The Thaw

for Marjorie Genevieve

W<small>ISDOM AFTER</small> *the event is a cheap enough commodity but* – go back.

The smoky light of a March sunrise is seeping through the winter drapes. Outside, the world is glassy, the trees on Pleasant Street glazed with winter. Every bare branch, every dead leaf is sheathed in ice, like a fossil from another age, an antediluvian dream of blossom and green canopies. Below her bedroom window, the drifts rise up in frozen waves of white – even the sudden gusts and eddies of wind cannot disturb those peaks – while overhead, the warmth of the sun is so reluctant in its offerings, so meagre, you'd not be alone if you failed to notice the coming of the first thaw.

Above her room, a sheet of ice on the eaves gives way, smashing like a minor glacier on to the porch roof, but everyone in the house sleeps on. Marjorie – or Marjorie Genevieve as her father always called her – sleeps in what the family still call Ethel's room, though it has been thirteen years since Ethel was taken from them by TB. Ethel, 1913. And Kathleen, just two years later. Marjorie still keeps one of Kathleen's Sunday handkerchiefs, spotted with her blood.

I

As for their mother, Cecelia Maud, it is true what people say. She has never recovered from the deaths of her three grown children: Ethel, Kathleen and, finally, senselessly, Murray, just two months after Kathleen. Before Christmas, Marjorie found her mother sitting in the ice-house with her coat unbuttoned and sawdust in her hair. Her lips were blue.

After seven daughters, Providence gave Cecelia Maud and James MacLeod a single son, a boy who would become the youngest lawyer ever admitted to the Bar in the province of Nova Scotia.

Some say the MacLeods hold themselves too high – which is perhaps why the fight broke out. At Batterson's, the bootlegger's. Between whom exactly, no one would ever say. Only this was clear: Murray was laid on the table in the so-called 'storeroom', a room anyone could see plainly by day, past the shop counter. Concussed, they said, that was all. Murray MacLeod would have a sorer head than usual come morning, and a hard time defending himself to his mother and his wife, lawyer or no. Louis Clarke, the town's inspector, gave them ten minutes while he turned a blind eye, stepped outside, and marvelled, as he was known to do, at the plenitude of stars in the Cape Breton sky. Two men – suddenly stark sober – heaved Murray into their arms. They took the short cut through Plant's Field; saw only the Portuguese fishermen who were camped, as ever, by the brook, their damp clothes hanging, pale as spectres, while their owners slept.

Cecelia Maud woke early. She planned to pick a few gem lettuces from the garden before they wilted in the day's heat. But, when she opened the inside door of the porch that close August morning, she found her only son

2

slumped against the rocker, blood still seeping from his ear.

Her legs gave way. Marjorie found her on the floor beside him.

But no charges were laid. No notice of the funeral was given in the church bulletin. It was 'family only'.

He was the youngest lawyer ever to be called to the Bar – dead after a night at the bootlegger's – and the MacLeods, Catholics, were not unaware: they were fortunate to reside on Pleasant Street, in the enviable Protestant district of Ward One.

Again.

Wisdom after the event is a cheap enough commodity – but the piece in the *North Sydney Herald* is still unimaginable, and as she wakes this Saturday morning Marjorie Genevieve is enjoying the knowledge that her coat was anything but cheap. She works Mondays and Wednesdays at the head office of Thompson's foundry. Before her father died, he made it clear he would consent only to a part-time position. She did not *need* to work, he explained with a benign smile, and although James MacLeod is now eight years gone, no one, not even Marjorie's eldest sister May, with her fierce intelligence and heavy eyebrows, has the authority to overturn his decision.

Marjorie knew it had to be beaver, not muskrat, not even muskrat dyed to look like mink.

A three-quarter-length, wrap-round coat in unsheared beaver.

She saved for two years.

In the darkness of her room, she slides it on over her nightgown and rubs her palm against the nape of the fur. The shawl collar tickles her bare neck. The silk lining is cool against her chest. When she pulls back the drapes, she can see almost nothing of the day through the bedroom window. The pane is a palimpsest of frost; the world is white. But she is radiantly warm.

She is twenty-nine, and it is only right. There has been enough grief.

Wearing the fur over only her nightgown, she feels nearly naked.

The furrier at Vooght Brothers had the voice of an orator. 'I do not need to persuade you of the elegance of this coat. But remember, while beaver is sometimes known for being heavy to wear, it offers *exceptional* protection against the excesses of a Cape Breton winter. Notice how the long guard-hairs give this coat its lustrous sheen.'

She noticed.

He took the liberty of easing the coat over her shoulders. The drape felt exquisite; the weight of the fur a strange new gravity. A lining of gold dress-silk flashed within. She wrapped the coat around herself, and felt the dense animal softness mould itself to her form.

'You won't find a more fashionable cut this side of Montreal.'

It was the coat of a mature woman, the coat of a woman of nearly thirty.

She deposited her payment in a small metal box and watched it whizz away on an electric wire. Within moments, the box came sailing back down the line, and revealed, as if by magic, her bill of sale.

Her account was settled.

The coat would be delivered.

The dance was Saturday night.

*   *   *

4

The penalties of past mistakes cannot be remitted, but at least the lessons so solemnly and dearly learned should be taken to heart.

But not yet. Wait –

because Charlie Thompson is pulling up next to the hitching-rail outside Vooght's, where William Dooley, the funeral director, has stopped his team. Steam rises from the horses' dark flanks as a small group of men – from Dooley's, the cable office, the Vendome Hotel, and the Royal Albert – gather to offer, with low whistles and eagle-eyes, their unreserved admiration for Charlie Thompson's new 1926 Buick Roadster.

Marjorie sees him – Mr Thompson, her employer – and nods briefly before turning right, when, in fact, she meant to turn left for home. But it is too late. Her pride in her new purchase has distracted her, and she doesn't want to walk past the group again straight away, so she slips into the Royal Café and orders tea with a slice of Lady Baltimore cake.

Outside the gleaming window, a single, tusky icicle drips, one of a long row that hangs from the café's awning, but Marjorie is unaware.

She watches, vaguely, the gathering of men across the street. William Dooley, the funeral director, has eased himself into the driver's seat. Mr Thompson is leaning on the door of the Buick, showing him the inner sanctum, but even so, he is taller than the others. She supposes he's handsome for a man of his age: dark-haired, grey only at the temples, a faltering sort of smile. Shame about the one short leg. A birth defect, she was told.

According to Eleanor in the office, he always walks fast, trying to disguise it, and his tailor 'gets hell' if the hems of his trousers don't skim the tops of his shoes. 'Maybe the bad leg's the reason he likes *speed*,' Eleanor murmured, leaning forward. 'Well, there's that new automobile, isn't there? Plus some fine breed of horse up at the racecourse.' She lowered her chin and whispered into her bosom, 'Apparently, he's a *gambler*.'

Maybe, thought Marjorie. But married, fifty, sober, Protestant, well-off, with three children. Respectable.

She leaves two bites of cake on her plate, as May taught her. She pushes in her chair, slips on her wool coat and pays the bill. Across the street, Charlie Thompson has resumed the ordinary shape of the man who lopes unevenly past her desk while the secretaries, Marjorie included, lower their heads out of courtesy.

As she slips through the door of the Royal Café, there can be no way for Marjorie to know that the man she is about to pass for the second time that day – Charlie Thompson, married, fifty, Protestant, with three children – is her future.

On Route 28, the chains on the car's tyres grip the snowy twists and bends. They hum, then clunk with every rotation, a primitive rhythm that sends Marjorie into a world of her own. It's a sixteen-mile journey from North Sydney to Sydney, and, wrapped in her new coat, she enjoys every moment, staring through her window at the frozen expanse of Sydney Harbour, mesmerised by its white, elemental glow.

So she makes only the poorest of efforts to shout over the engine for chit-chat with Eleanor and her brother Tom up front. The forty-minute journey passes in what seems like ten, and in no time the flaming tower of Sydney's steelworks looms into view, spitting like a firework about to explode.

The *Herald* will assure us that, as she arrives at the Imperial Hotel on Sydney's Esplanade, Marjorie is *a young lady* whose thoughts are *centred on an evening's innocent recreation*. In the lobby, she passes her fur to the cloakroom attendant, wondering if the girl will be tempted to try it on when no one's looking. *Go on*, she wants to say. *I don't mind*! But she doesn't want to presume.

'Don't forget your dance cards!' the girl calls after them, and Marjorie dashes back.

The names of the dances marked on the cards make her and Eleanor laugh: the Turkey Trot, the Wiggle-de-Wiggle, the Shorty George, the Necktie Waltz, the Fuzzy Wuzzy . . . Sixteen in all. 'I hope I've got a little Negro in my blood,' shouts Eleanor as they sashay into the ballroom. Marjorie can only force a smile, not knowing the polite reply. Besides, the twelve-man band is already bugling and strumming, swaying and tromboning, and Marjorie knows this one – 'Everything's Gonna Be All Right'.

'There must be more than five hundred people here,' marvels Eleanor.

Marjorie is swapping her boots for her Mary Janes. 'And half from North Sydney!'

'I told you we wouldn't be stuck with Tom all night. Besides, there are enough men from the KOC to mean that even the Pope himself would approve of our Turkey Trot. Look! Mr Thompson's here too.'

Marjorie spots him, smoking near the rear door. She shrugs.

But Eleanor is still squinting. 'He's here with the racecourse set.'

Marjorie turns to the band. Five of the twelve men are black. Two, the deepest black. She's heard there are Negro families in Sydney who've come all the way from the Deep South.

She's only ever seen a Negro once in North Sydney, a stoker from the foundry who came into the office because his wages were overdue. She liked the sound of his voice; the lazy music of his words.

Eleanor yells over the band, 'He's come on his own.'

'Who has?'

'Mrs Thompson isn't here. Not that it matters! He never dances anyway with that short leg of his.'

Marjorie can see Tom crossing the floor towards them, refreshments in hand. In a moment, thankfully, Eleanor will have another ear.

'Though you never know.' She giggles and tugs at Marjorie's sleeve. 'The Shorty George might be just the number for him!'

Marjorie knows she should, but she doesn't care enough about Mr Thompson to protest on his behalf. Besides, it's a new song now, one she's never heard – 'If You Can't Land Her On The Ol' Verandah' – and beneath her satin dress, her hips are already swaying as if they had a life of their own.

Time is flying – she has no notion of the hour. She's red-faced and giddy from dancing too much, and the room still heaves with dancers. Even Joe 'Clunk' McEwan is stepdancing on a table-top to 'The Alabama Stomp'.

Someone has propped open the rear doors for a blast of cold winter air, and hip flasks of bootlegged whisky are passing from man to man across the dance floor. The MC is starting to slur, and the twelve-man band is three men down, but the music roars on.

She plucks her dress away from her to catch any breath of air.

'Excuse me, Miss. Is there room for one more on your dance card?'

Marjorie turns. One of the Negro men from the band – the double-bass player – is standing before her, his shoulders back, his tie loose at his neck.

Eleanor's hand flies to her chest. Tom takes a step forward.

Marjorie can see the man is not drunk. His eyes are clear, his gaze steady. For a moment, she wishes he were. She might know what to do. She extends her hand. 'I'm enjoying the music.'

He nods, grinning at the parquet floor. 'I'm Walter. Would you like to dance, Miss?'

'Marjorie.' She clasps her palms. 'But I have to confess, Walter, I'm done in for the night.'

He clicks his tongue. 'A fine dancer like you? Why, you just need your second wind.'

She risks it. 'I'm sure it's none of my business, Walter, but are you one of the steelworkers from down South?' *Are the nights sultry?* she wants to ask. *Do the women carry fans?*

He nods. 'From Alabama, Miss.'

She wishes he would call her Marjorie. 'But Sydney's your home now?'

'Not Sydney proper, Miss.'

'No?'

'No.' He runs a hand across his chin and searches her face. 'Me and my family live in Cokeville.'

She smiles politely. Then it comes to her: Cokeville. The area by Whitney Pier, where the run-off from the coke ovens pours into the estuary.

The band strikes up a waltz, 'Wistful and Blue'. Walter offers her his hand. She is surprised by the pale flesh of his palms.

She can feel the eyes of many more than Tom and Eleanor now. But his hand still waits, and the truth is, she *would* like to dance.

As she takes his hand, she can feel the calluses on his fingertips. She has never met a double-bass player before. Up close, he smells of lye, like the bar her mother keeps by the set-tub. From the seating area there arises a low drone of disapproval.

Couple after couple leave the dance floor.

She reaches after conversation, speaking into his ear. 'So you brought your family with you to Sydney?'

He leads well. 'Yes, that's right. My mamma and my sisters.'

She dreads the eye of the roaming spotlight. 'That must be difficult – with just you to look after them, I mean.'

She can see his eyes assessing the risk: is it better to lead her into the shadows of the ballroom or to keep to the bright centre? 'Yes, Miss, I do my best. But it's been especially hard since my brother was killed.'

'Killed?' She stops dancing.

''Fraid so. Just before we left Alabama. At a speak-easy in our town. Leonard was hired to wash glasses. But a fight broke out over something or other that had gone missing. The manager was drunk. Went mad as a hornet. Broke a glass – on purpose like – and cut Leonard's throat.'

The shape of her brother Murray rises in Marjorie's mind's eye. Blood still seeps from his ear.

'Did they get the man, Walter, or did he get away?'

'Neither, Miss. They didn't get the man – and he didn't get away.' He swallows. 'That was hard, for my mamma especially.'

Marjorie nods, and she remembers her mother, alone in the ice-house, her lips blue.

Out of the corner of her eye, she notices that several of the men from the KOC have risen from their chairs and stand, watching. They're wondering if Walter has offended her; if that's why she's having words. So she smiles at her partner, to say she is ready to dance again, and Walter waltzes her back to the centre of the floor.

On stage, the MC is fiddling with his cuffs and trying, without success, to catch the eye of the conductor. 'Blue and Wistful' floats on into the wintery night – *one*, two, three – while the ballroom of the Imperial Hotel empties. The KOC men, Marjorie notices, haven't sat back down in their chairs, and Walter's hand has gone cold in hers.

A voice sounds at the dark edge of the spotlight: 'Excuse me.'

Walter stops short. Marjorie squeezes her eyes shut. She can feel the air around her about to break.

'May I?'

She opens her eyes. Charlie Thompson is standing before them. He has tapped Walter's shoulder.

Walter nods, then smiles, blinking too much, before he thanks Marjorie for the dance. Marjorie presses his forearm. 'Thank you for asking.' He makes for the safety of the stage as Charlie Thompson takes her hand in his. She feels his other hand, light on the small of her back. His face tenses as he strains to pick out the beat. Then they step into the mercy of darkness, his bad leg stammering.

When he returns her to her table, Eleanor is talking to Jimmy Monaghan. She doesn't turn to acknowledge Marjorie.

Charlie Thompson hovers, his head bowed. 'Thank you for the dance, Marjorie. It was kind of you to put up with my two left feet.'

'Thank *you*, Mr Thompson.' She has to look away so the tears don't come.

He glances at the backs of Eleanor and Jimmy Monaghan. 'I'm driving back to North Sydney now, in case you need a lift.'

She turns to the table and tries again. 'Eleanor?'

But Eleanor pretends not to hear. So Marjorie finds her clutch on the floor and tries to smile. 'Thank you. It *is* very late.'

Outside, the snow that was falling earlier has turned to sleet, and word has it that the roads are slick. As she bundles herself into the Buick, she hardly knows what possesses her. 'Cokeville.' She stares into her lap. 'Before we go back, Mr Thompson, would you show me Cokeville?'

His hand hovers over the gearbox. Out of courtesy, he tries to sound breezy. 'Sure. It's not so far out of our way.'

She smells it before she sees it: a stink of slag and human sewage. Under the angry candle of the steelworks tower, rows of dark bunkhouses and shacks appear in the night.

Charlie Thompson turns off the engine.

She stumbles into speech. 'But Bill at the foundry said these men are skilled labourers. I thought that's why they were asked to come all this way.'

'Yes.'

'I thought all the steelworkers and their families lived in the Ashby area.'

'Not all – sadly.'

Marjorie pulls her coat tight. Charlie lights a cigarette for her. But she suspects her hand will shake if she tries to hold it.

He rubs the windshield clear of the mist of their breath. 'It's after midnight, Marjorie.'

'Of course. I'm keeping you, and my mother will be waiting up.'

In the narrow space of the two-door Buick, he turns to her for the first time, and winks. 'Not to mention the fact that you'll catch hell from your big sister when she hears. I see her very . . . patient husband up at the track.'

She lets herself laugh.

'We'll take the harbour, shall we?' he says. 'Make up a bit of lost time?'

She sits up in her seat, surfacing from the depths of her coat. 'Tom, Eleanor's brother, said the harbour is risky now.'

Charlie casts his cigarette into the night. 'I came that way. The ice was rock solid.' He smiles. 'You don't think I'd play fast and loose with this baby, do you?' He thumps the steering wheel, then releases the clutch.

A *gambler*, said Eleanor. 'Apparently, he's a *gambler*.' Of course, he'd have to be to offer her a lift home in the first place. Not that she had to accept. Maybe that makes them two of a kind. She only knows that it's past midnight and that it will be a slow crawl back to North Sydney by road.

She wonders what she'll say to her mother and May when word gets out – about Walter; about the lateness of the hour; about Mr Thompson, married and Protestant.

At Muggah's Creek, the new 1926 Buick Roadster glides on to the ice.

But even now, there's time. Will she say it?

Shall we turn back? Everyone says you shouldn't cross after the 1st of March.

No.

Because what's five days to twenty inches of ice, and hasn't it been snowing most of the night? Besides, it's just eight miles. In a quarter of an hour, they'll be landing on the sandbar at Indian Beach.

She has never crossed by night before. The swollen sky bears down on them. In the wide, dark limbo of Sydney Harbour, the Buick's headlamps seem no brighter than a pair of jack-o'-lanterns.

Every year the Council says it will provide range-lights and a few bush-marked courses, but the owners of the ice-breakers protest. How will they clear the harbour's shipping lane with lights, markers and more traffic to circumnavigate?

As the car moves out across the frozen estuary, Charlie Thompson's hands are rigid on the wheel. Now and again, the car fantails, but he pulls it back into line and on they go.

She'll laugh on the other side. Perhaps she'll even have one of Mr Thompson's cigarettes or a swig from his flask to steady her nerves.

She would lay her head back and close her eyes – she's so tired now – but cold air blasts through the windows. Mr Thompson says they have to stay open so they don't fog up.

And suddenly, for no reason, she remembers the old Micmac woman who came to the door selling coloured baskets. 'I'm sorry,' the woman said, taking Marjorie's mother's thin hand in her own. 'I am sorry about your three daughters.'

How did she know?

But 'No,' said Marjorie, coming to her mother's aid. 'My mother has lost two daughters and the son of the house. *Two* daughters. Three children. But thank you for your condolences.' And the woman looked at her – looked right *through* her – before turning away.

She shakes herself. They are almost clear of the estuary. Another ten minutes and they'll be on terra firma. She tries to brighten. 'All things considered,' she says, turning to Charlie Thompson, 'I enjoyed myself tonight.'

He laughs, relieved to have conversation. 'I haven't danced so much in years.'

'You danced half of one dance!'

'Exactly. My wife will never believe it.'

She doesn't look at him as she says it. 'You'll tell your wife then.'

He leans forward, mopping the windshield with his sleeve. 'Haven't decided yet. I have a policy, you might say. I try my damnedest to live in the moment.'

She nods, as if his reply were neither here nor there.

'Which means,' he says, winking again, 'I'll think about it tomorrow when I'm sitting in church.'

'Where you can calmly resolve to think about it later!'

'Bullseye.'

She settles back into her seat, laughing. She recalls again the easy sway of her hips as she danced, and Walter's firm arm leading, and Mr Thompson bending over her, tall, close, protective. She starts to hum a few bars from one of the tunes. From behind the wheel, Charlie Thompson catches her eye and joins in, stringing together a few lines from the refrain. He has a fine voice, she says to herself –

when the car goes through the ice.

The hole opens like a black mouth. The Buick tips – her hands can't find the handle – and suddenly, unfathomably, the car is locked in jaws of ice.

The headlamps are out, and she can't tell if the space above her is the window that faces up or down. His or hers. There's no top, no bottom, no floor, no roof, no ocean bed, no ice hole. *Mr Thompson?* Water is rushing across her lap – *my new coat, my coat* – and her mind can't catch up.

I tell myself this.

She feels his hand grabbing at her shoulder – *thank God*, she thinks, *thank God*. He's hauling her up by the collar of her coat, and she's pushing off with her feet, gulping air. Is that his voice calling or the groaning of steel against ice?

But the car shifts again, a wave churns through, and –

No.

The car is falling, juddering, through the ice. *Mr Thompson!*

But he's nowhere.

Such darkness. Such cold. Like she has never known.

Her coat clings, sodden. Heavy.

Unimaginably heavy.

A dead animal weight.

And the Micmac woman is beside her in the footwell – *sssh now, quiet* – as the car sinks to the bottom of the estuary.

In the article in the *Herald*, she will remain unnamed. A kindness perhaps.

There will be no obituary.

In the years to come, no one will be christened in her memory.

Sometimes, I tell people about my great-aunt who went under the ice.

ALEXANDRA FOX

Whalebone Stays

IN A quiet, cool room, Ann sits and sews. Her office is carved uncomfortably from the great hall of Avebury House, Museum of Social History, home of the Mercer Collection of Corsetry. If Ann were to look up, she would see, partitioned by hardboard, the belly of a painted cherub, a fragment of gilded cornicing.

But Ann does not look up. She wears magnifying spectacles on her pointy nose (her chin is small and pointy too, as are her elbows), and the focus of the lenses extends only to the six inches or so of worn fabric in her embroidery hoop. Ann is reattaching the delicate lace edging to a Victorian child's nightdress. She draws a fine strand from a contemporaneous handkerchief, threads it into her needle and darns, working over and under, to and fro, until her stitches form a weave of their own, immaculate, almost imperceptible.

When the door opens, Ann removes her glasses. Philip Gregson enters, dragging a leather trunk.

'A delivery for Miss Anastasia,' he says, with a mock-courtly bow.

The first time the Director used her Christian name was at her job interview, when she was fresh out of college. 'But it says here that your name is Anastasia Dubovie . . .' She hadn't heard it said, said in a man's deep voice, for ten years or more.

'Anastasia,' he'd repeated. 'I don't understand. A name so rich and romantic, so full of the sweep of history, but you call yourself Ann ... an indefinite article.' She'd withered into her seat.

Philip drops a key on to the desk. Ann looks at the dark hairs curling on his wrist, his green-velvet sleeve. She itches to fix loose stitching at the seam, but the intimacy of the suggestion lies out of reach of her tongue.

'Don't work too late,' he says, and leaves.

The decaying leather of the trunk stains Ann's hands with a fine red dust. The lock has rusted. It is a donation – attic clutter from a woman wanting to open up the roof-space in her Victorian town house. 'It's full of old underwear and stuff. Would it be any use to the Museum?'

The 'underwear' consists of a full set of corsets, scarcely worn, wrapped in brittle silk. There are Symington Morn and Noon corsets, the morning version cut lower under the arms for easier reach (they have a set in the Collection already, but these are in better condition); a long, thick calfskin corset, heavily boned, the leather crumbling slightly; there's a set of sleeping-stays in reinforced white cambric. The gem of the collection is an evening corset, set with twenty-four whalebone strips, decorated with gold feather stitching, ribbons and floss. It is yellow with starch, steam moulded until it stands alone, and the waist is impossibly small.

Among the 'stuff' is a diary, bound in dove-grey kid. Ann opens it. 'Henrietta Wylmington, Avebury Square, England, 1883' is written in a looped cursive hand, childlike and regular. The ink has a coppery sheen.

14 September. Today is my thirteenth birthday! How wonderful! I finally received my corsets. I feel much of

the elation still. Immediately when the corsetière drew my laces in, I could tell I would enjoy them; the feel of their tightness against my skin & the new posture induced is most pleasing. My sisters have cautioned me not to incline Mamma to lace me into the most restrictive set, although I am very curious about how they feel . . .

Ann remembers her own thirteenth birthday – no quiet family celebration (no siblings), no visit to the cinema with a few close friends (no close friends). Without asking, her mother had invited the entire school class 'for tea' . . . those Ann had never spoken to, those who despised her, those she hid from. The garden doors were thrown open; tables were filled with food and flowers; jolly music played. And as the almost guestless afternoon progressed Ann withered in a corner until her mother phoned her own exuberant friends to join her for an impromptu feast.

Ann puts the diary into her canvas bag. She will begin transcribing it on her laptop at home. She picks up her coat. Then she stops, turns back to the trunk, takes out the Morn corset, and tucks it hurriedly into her bag.

Ann leaves the Museum through panelled halls, silent but not empty. Painted eyes stare at her from glass cases. Plaster figures pose in crinolines and farthingales of the long dead. Perhaps it is the fleeting memory of a story Daddy once told her – about dolls that sprang to life while she slept – but Ann sometimes thinks that, as she locks the doors behind her, bewigged heads will leap on to headless bodies; stockinged legs will knit themselves to corseted torsos. And the ancient halls will teem with storytelling, under the benevolent eyes of the Jesuit seminarian found suffocated by the safety of his own priest's hole, the sacred vessels clutched against his ribs for three hundred years.

Home then, to the shadow of the elephant.

Ann has the ground floor to herself. It is uncluttered, with sisal carpets and white walls. She has a small television for the news, a steel work table and sewing machine, a single wing chair. The bookshelves house necessary books – French and Italian dictionaries, standard works on costume, authoritative biographies of historical figures, directories of makers' marks. And, tucked in a low corner, despite everything, well-thumbed copies of *The House at Pooh Corner* and *The Tailor of Gloucester*.

As she opens the fridge, the ceiling joists creak. A breathless voice calls down, 'Annie darling, is that you? Back so early? Come, tell me about your day.'

Upstairs, Mother's room is stuffed with Mother. Her bulk is too wide for the doorway, too heavy for the stairs. She overhangs the reinforced double bed. She is whale-like in the smooth curves of her blubber, amorphous, spreading to engulf everything within reach – books, radio, paints, telephone, friends, daughter – integrating them into her body. Her incongruously pretty face floats on top, like a cherry on a Belgian bun.

For five years, Mother has shifted no further than the patent Japanese commode beside her bed, which swishes warm water at her vast bottom, dries it with hot air and puffs of baby-powder. She calls it her sumo-bog.

Ann lifts folds of skin on her mother's belly and hips and under her pendulous breasts, wipes away sweat and replaces clean sheets of gauze beneath them, as impersonally as the placing of tissue paper between layers of antique fabric. She rocks her, side to side, until they have gained enough momentum to tip. Ann checks her back and buttocks, rubs alcohol on oozing pressure sores. She tries not to look at the purple stain across her shoulder, the tattoo of 'Anastasia' stretched into illegibility.

'We're chalk and cheese,' her mother told her once.

'In that case, I'm the stick of chalk, and you're the oozy Brie.'

'We've just got to keep looking for calcium.'

'Calcium?'

'When you've got two things as different as chalk and cheese you've just got to look for the good they've got in common,' her mother said. 'And that's calcium.'

If Ann regrets anything, it is the period between eighteen and twenty-two stone when her mother would catch sight of herself in a shop window and ask, 'Do I really look like that, darling?' and she should have shaken her until her belly wobbled and shouted, 'Yes! Yes, you do!' But she blames herself no longer for the inexorable swelling of the elephant. She provides three healthy, nourishing meals a day, calorie-counted for an inactive woman in her fifties. Then she leaves for work, and she knows (for she has watched from the corner) that a steady stream of her mother's friends will arrive throughout the day, with bottles of sherry, DVDs, sandwiches and cakes, conversation and laughter. How can they bear that fetid room, the suffocating toomuchness of her?

Today, Ann finds herself talking about Henrietta's diary.

'That's a wicked thing to do to a young girl,' her mother says.

'Why? She says she's elated.'

'Oh Annie. Think of the damage she did to her body, distorting her ribs, squeezing up her organs. I bet she could hardly breathe. I'd never let a daughter of mine restrict herself like that.'

'I know.' Ann remembers her childhood home (after Daddy left and the laces of their life were untied), the upper floors let out to lodgers ... the constant noise, the mess, trying to concentrate on homework at one end of the long kitchen table while her mother stirred and whisked at the other, catering for receptions and other people's freezers. She remembers the idiosyncratic clothes passed on from older children, the sniggering at parents' evenings as her mother's bulk overflowed the classroom chairs. Her mother never stopped offering. She just couldn't understand when it wasn't wanted ... doughy, sweaty hugs – or food, pressed on her, piled on her plate, until Ann would hide potatoes in her napkin, flush bread surreptitiously down the lavatory, drop her breakfast into a bin on the way to school.

Later, naked in the privacy of her bedroom, Ann examines the machine-stitching on the Victorian corset; she tests its strength with her hands. She slackens the laces to their loosest extent. She attempts to fasten the busk around her front but the studs and clasps will not meet. She's a petite size eight. She has no excess fat. How can it not close?

She soaks the fabric, lies on the bed and forces it around her body, like a 1960s teenager in new Levi's. When she rolls herself upright she feels sick and faint. She feels elated.

Ann wears the corset until it has fully dried and the starch has set into her own body-shape. She measures her waist as twenty-three inches. She discovers that she must hold herself straight, that any slouching or hunching of the shoulders makes the corset cut under her arms. When she takes it off before bed, she discovers dark-purple bruises along her lower ribs. But still she is exhilarated.

Over the next weeks she monitors the reduction of her waist. In spare moments, she manipulates her lower ribs, loosening their attachment to her spine. She finds the pace frustratingly slow, unlike Henrietta, whose diary documents a tightening of an inch per week. But then Henrietta was thirteen to Ann's twenty-nine years, her skeleton more malleable. And Henrietta had the advantage of a mother who took her seriously.

24 September. We aggravated Mamma at luncheon and after a harsh scolding she laced each of us into our correction corsets. I could tell it would be confining, from low below my hip bones to pinching high in my armpits. Just when I thought she was done tightening my laces she instructed me to stretch to my toes & grasp as high as possible on my bedpost, then harshly laced me down another two inches . . . I feel fatigued after an almost sleepless night. With any exertion I feel as if my breath has been robbed.

Ann slips the cambric sleeping-stays into her bag and brings them home from the conservators' workroom. They are stiffened with hemp cords rather than whalebone and reach from her small breasts to low on her hips. The first night she wears them, she finds herself trapped log-like in the bed, unable to turn or roll. She wakes in the dark, fighting in panic for each shallow breath.

And that's when she senses Daddy, sitting at the end of the bed (though she'd promised herself, after finding *that* picture, that she'd dream of him no longer). She's eleven again. She smells his woody cologne, feels the strong tightness as he tucks her into a 'boat' of cool sheets. She hears him as he sounded that last time, uncharacteristically hesitant, his faint accent. 'It isn't you, Anastasia. Believe me. You're the most important thing in my life. It's your mother; I can't bear to live with her any more. That's why I stay away, why I'm leaving. You know how she is ... always noise and fuss, friends in and out, wine, supper parties. There's no order, no peace. Wait just a year or two, my darling, and I'll send for you. I'll miss you so very much ...' She feels the traitorous brush of his moustache on her forehead as he kisses her goodbye.

The first time Ann wears the corset to the Museum, she covers it with a loose smock. She has developed strategies for sitting and walking. She has learnt to bend from the knees rather than the waist, though she is still unable to pick things up off the floor without kneeling.

She is laced to only twenty inches. She's achieved nineteen inches at home with the aid of a button-hook, but knows that a full day sitting at a desk will cause her liver to ache.

If anyone comments about her posture, she will say that she is wearing a medical brace. She's overheard the security staff saying she has 'a poker up her arse', so this will do nothing to change their perception of her. She watches them sometimes in the courtyard – guides and guards alike – eating pasties from greasy bags, smoking, nipping off for a pint. She cannot understand how they can act like this; they are custodians of their heritage. Ann brings a lunch box from home, a small white sandwich of Edam or chicken roll and cucumber, a Golden Delicious apple, a bottle of spring water. She eats at her desk, then washes her hands before returning to her work.

Philip, the Director, visits her in her workroom. He

is wearing a navy blazer, lilac shirt, bow tie. His neat Vandyke beard is darker than his hair.

'I know you're not one to put yourself forward,' he says, 'but I wonder if you might help me.'

Ann quickly removes her glasses. She looks up at him. In five years he has rarely sustained a conversation with her. So why now?

'It's an idea I had for the festival. I thought we might hold a Living History evening, here in the Museum. We could bring in a harpist; a good friend of mine plays the harpsichord. We could serve some authentic recipes. And I wondered if . . . if . . .'

'You want me to give a talk about the costumes?'

'Yes, but more than that. Dresses behind glass aren't really "living history", are they? I wondered if you might agree to display one or two of the outfits – wear them yourself – those that are robust enough, obviously. Let people understand the difficulties of walking, going through doors, the posture imposed by the fashions.'

'Wouldn't an actress do it better?' Ann asks.

'Maybe. But they wouldn't have your knowledge.' He smiles down at her. 'And I don't know why . . . but there's something about you that isn't of this century. Would you think about it?'

'Yes, Philip.'

When the east wind blows, dead fingers of wisteria rattle and tap at the bedroom windows. Confined by her rigid stays, Ann cannot burrow under the duvet to escape their accusatory whispers. She remembers the weight of indigo blossoms that festooned the house each May, and passers-by stopping with cameras. She remembers the summer they started to turn brown and papery.

Her mother had noticed too. 'Annie,' she said through her bedroom doorway, like Pooh stuck on the wrong side of Rabbit's hole. 'That wisteria should have another fifty years in it, easy. Check the wall-ties on the main stem. One of them must be too tight, cutting off the sap.'

So Ann traced the woody branches as they rambled over the brickwork. She refastened clips and twists. It wasn't until she brushed compost from the very base of the plant that she discovered the original name-tag, 'Blue Rain', on a wire band so tight that the wood had distorted around it and sap oozed from the damaged stem. And she took hold of that wire and twisted it tighter still.

But that was during the bad summer, the summer when she cut the letter-box string so her mother's friends couldn't let themselves in with the key. It was the summer when she discovered her mother lowering a basket out of the window with a list of goodies (the neighbourhood kids treated her as some sort of sacred monster in her mammoth obesity, and did not steal her money), the summer Ann nailed that window shut through sweaty August days and nights. It was the summer of that photograph.

Her mother ran a business from her bed, painting cakes. She worked with a palette of edible colourings and hair-fine paintbrushes, producing glowing frescoes on a canvas of royal icing. She worked from memory and imagination, often from photographs for specific commissions.

They didn't take *Country Life*. It was only in the house for a photograph of Cowdrey Towers which her mother was copying for an anniversary cake. Ann thumbed through it idly, glancing at the pictures.

She stopped. Daddy. His moustache was the same, but he'd added a small beard on the point of his chin. His hair was greying.

The bride beside him glowed.

Ann read the caption: 'How can he bear to give her away? Stefan Dubovie at the wedding of his daughter Annoushka, 22. The bride wears head-to-toe Castigliano in ivory duchesse satin ...'

'You're the most important thing in my life ... Wait just a year or two, my darling, and I'll send for you.' And all the time he had another life, secret from them both, another daughter, a tall, beautiful, laughing daughter ... his Annoushka ... his Little Ann.

So where did the inadequacy lie? In her loud, gross mother. Or in herself?

By the Evening of Living History, Ann has achieved a seventeen-inch waist. Fully laced, her boyish figure sprouts breasts and buttocks. She wears Elastoplast over sores where her ribs and hip bones are almost visible through the skin.

She has had the free run of the Collection, a choice of corsets with names like Queen Bess, Bird's Wing, La Graciosa. She decides to dress in the wasp-waisted fashions of the 1890s, a sturdy whalebone corset in khaki coutil worn under a tea dress of pink brocade with creamy flounces. It is an occasion when she needs female assistance. For evening parties, Henrietta's corsetière would treat her 'with wonderful detail, carefully lacing & adjusting the fit', but Ann manages alone, painfully, with the hook on the back of the lavatory door and a long shoe-horn.

When she comes into the hall, the harpsichordist is already playing something intricate and baroque, Jacobean lace hanging at his wrists. Tapestry banners spill their dust gently on to the panelling. There is a scent of beeswax candles, of polish and pastry, of expectation, of age. She breathes it all in, with short, shallow breaths.

Hands encircle her waist from behind. It is Philip (she can smell the sandalwood oil he uses on his hair). She does not turn.

'My dear Anastasia,' he murmurs into her neck. 'So this is what you hide away under those boring clothes. It's extraordinary. I can touch my fingers around your waist. And your hair is quite marvellous.'

Ann turns her head and looks up at him. She is perfectly aware of the fullness of her bosom. The dumpy curator and the cheap-voiced girl from the Museum shop watch from the doorway. Surely they must see his hands, her tiny waist, his hands upon her waist. She lengthens her neck, lifts her chin, and her forehead brushes against his neat, dark beard. His hazel eyes reflect the soft green of the old velvet jacket. She can understand why Victorian women 'swooned' with emotion. It is only the restriction, she tells herself, the pressure of bone on heart and lung.

Ann isn't sure whether she's a virgin. There was a humiliating episode in college with a fellow misfit, but he said that she had 'something wrong with her down there'. She believed him; she shrank helplessly into herself. But now she has watched television, read books. She wonders if the tightness he complained of might have been due to his fumbling inexperience rather than any deficiency of her own. She fearfully desires an older, kind, experienced man to reassure her.

Ann stations herself beside the cases of corsetry. Someone hands her a glass of white wine. A harp strums softly. She explains the manufacture of the garments, the capture of the Russian whales whose bones support their great bulk under pressure of deep water. She laughingly fastens stays around buxom women; she traces the history of knickers and bras for giggling schoolgirls; she shows off her own tight-lacing, how difficult it is to bend and breathe. She reads to them from Henrietta's diary, the last pathetic entry in June, where she fearfully tells of her sister's smallpox.

And each time she laughs or smiles or jokes, she looks over at Philip.

The evening winds down. The harpist leaves. There are sounds of washing-up and doors closing.

Ann is replacing gloves in their cases when she hears Philip's voice behind her.

'You were wonderful tonight,' he says. 'A shame for it to end. I don't suppose you'd like to come for a drink?'

She gasps. 'Philip, I'd love to.' She speaks clearly. The stout curator and the shop girl are still putting on their coats. She smiles, turns.

'Good show. We'll be in the White Hart if you fancy it.' His arm is draped around the neck of his good friend the harpsichord player. 'Rafa won't mind if you join us, will you, old boy . . . just for one?'

Ann waits. She walks through the panelled halls, silent but not empty. Painted faces smirk from glass cases. The Jesuit seminarian is not benevolent at all.

Home, and her mother's calling down the stairs, asking how the evening went.

Ann goes straight through to her bedroom. She shuts the door, draws the curtains tight. The eye-bolt is ready, fixed to a strong joist in the ceiling. All she needs to do is pass the rope through it.

She strips and takes the evening corset from its silken

shroud. The boning is fine and delicate, the gold embroidery exquisite.

Ann fastens the wooden busk under her breasts, hooks the loops around the metal studs. She ties the ends of the back-laces to the door handle.

Then she stands on the bed, grips hold of the lacing trapeze that she has hung from the ceiling, and leans forward with her entire body. The corset tightens. Eighteen inches, and her ribs are straining away from her spine. Seventeen inches, and the bile rises in her mouth from her displaced stomach. Ann is diminishing herself, becoming less than a whole.

Sixteen . . . Even triple-stitching of the finest order isn't eternal. Over the past hundred years it's thinned and weakened. Now it parts, splits, tears. It gives, completely. The bolt rips from the ceiling. Ann flies forward. She smacks her face against the brass headboard.

Upstairs, there is a sound of rhythmic creaking, so loud it seems the joists will crack. Mother is rocking, forward and back, forward and back, gaining momentum to rise from her bed.

The mountain is on the move.

But it's Ann who gets to the stairs first, bleeding from nose and broken mouth, the corset flapping round her. She runs up to her mother, who's forcing herself through the bedroom doorway, weeping helplessly.

She burrows herself into her mother's fatness, feels the good constriction of those vast arms enveloping her, the smell of powder and sweat and cake.

'Oh Mum,' she says. She lets out the breath she's been holding all her life. 'Don't let me go.'

NORA MORRISON

All for the Best

WE'RE BORED, so we chap on Mrs Duggan's door and ask if we can mind Joe for her. She likes it when we take him into the back green. 'Joe, pet, would you like to go out for a wee while wi' Margaret an' Doreen?' Joe doesn't understand, so she nods for him and he nods too.

'It's good for him, the poor soul, to see the sun,' she tells us.

'You two be sure to mind my Joe, now!' Mrs Duggan flaps her hands, motioning us towards the stairs, eager to get on with her housework uninterrupted. The glossy white door of her flat closes. We look up at Joe. Joe smiles down at us, uncertain.

'It's a' right, Joe, you're comin' out to play wi' us.'

We beckon him to follow us down the stairs. He does so, hesitantly at first, his big hands clinging to the wooden banister as though it were a lifeline back to his mammy. The Duggans live at number 8, right on the top floor of our tenement, so it takes us a while to coax him right down to the back close.

We hold his hands to lead him out into the back green, where he lifts his face to the sun. Eyelids screwed up tight against the glare, he grins with pleasure. The grass is thin, in places giving way to hard-packed earth, muddy where hollows have formed. We lead Joe towards the wash-

31

house, where green-painted poles mark the boundaries of the drying area. I tie one end of our rope around one of the poles and put the other end in Joe's hand. He knows what to do. He grins and swings the rope up and around, and we take turns at skipping. Joe never wants a turn. Up and around, up and around goes the rope until we tire and catch hold of it.

We find a patch of good grass in the sun for Joe to sit on. He minds our dollies for us while we play hide-and-seek with the boys. We tried playing hide-and-seek with Joe once, but he got scared when he couldn't find us, and he started to moan, quietly at first, then louder. We heard a window on the top floor squeal open and Mrs Duggan stuck her head out. She jabbed her finger in my direction.

'Margaret Kerr, don't you be teasin' our Joe or I'll tell your mammy on you!'

So we try hard not to make Joe moan.

Once I ask, 'Mammy, why's Joe Duggan a poor soul?'

Mammy is making jam. Rows of newly cleaned jam-jars glint, all shapes and sizes, set out for inspection on the kitchen table like soldiers on parade; near by, a heap of greaseproof papers and brown elastic bands waiting at the ready to complete the operation. Gently, I shuffle the greaseproof circles into a tall column.

'Away and don't bother me.' Mammy is at the cooker, slowly stirring a big pan with a long wooden spoon. The sweet-tart smell of teatimes fills the warm air.

'But why, Mammy?' I tug at the strings of her pinny.

Mammy turns to frown down at me. The headscarf which covers her brown hair is twisted around her head and secured by a knot on top, and beads of sweat cling to her brow.

'Because he's no' right in the heid.' She turns back to the steaming pot.

'Whit's wrang wi' his heid, Mammy?'

She shakes her head and mumbles something about it being wrong to have children late in life. 'And who'll look efter 'im when she's gone, that's whit Ah'd like to know.'

'Doreen an' me. We look efter 'im. But whit's wrang wi' his heid, Mammy?'

'He's daft, that's whit.' She tuts loudly. 'Wains! Whit will ye be askin' next? Away out now!'

Joe's thick finger delicately traces the greens and golds on the embossed border that bisects the white tiles of the close. Doreen and I ponder over the question of Joe's head and what might not be right with it. But that summer he serves our purposes well. We feel proud to have a grown-up for a friend, and we know the boys are jealous. Mrs Duggan won't let the boys take Joe out to play since they made him climb on top of the back-court wall and he got stuck. Now they shout names at Joe when they think his mammy won't hear them. Eric says Joe was a soldier in the war. He got shrapnel in his head when he was fighting the Jerries and that's why he's daft. Shrapnel is bits of metal, Eric says. We get Joe to sit on the bottom step so we can climb up behind him and look at his head, but we can't see shrapnel. Just a shiny pink line where his hair doesn't grow.

The bins are enclosed by brick walls so you don't see them. Mammy says the midden is dirty and we mustn't play there. But the big metal bins hold treasures we can use for playing shops, or houses. We creep close, holding our noses against the cloying smell of decay. The bin lids gape open with the volume of rubbish inside, and wasps hover lazily around the rims. We are too small to peer inside.

We take Joe by the hand and pull him towards the nearest bin. He doesn't mind the eggshells and bits of tomato and squashes them underfoot. We flick the wasps aside, hold the rim, try to pull the bin over. It stands firm, but Joe understands now. He grasps the bin firmly. There is a loud clatter as metal hits concrete; slops, mess and muck cascade out, thick dust puffs into the air.

Faces appear at windows: Mrs McPherson, Mrs Brown, Mrs Sinclair squint through the glass. Mrs McWhirter from number 3 pulls up her kitchen window.

'Whit's goin' on doon there?' she bellows. We are hidden from her view, but Joe is tall and she can see his head and shoulders above the midden wall.

'Get you away from there!' she yells at him. 'Wait till your mammy hears, Joe Duggan!'

We creep outside the midden and wait while Mrs Duggan comes scurrying down from the fourth floor. Joe is still standing among the bins, his shoes peeping through a heap of potato peelings and wet tea leaves.

'It was Joe, Mrs Duggan, honest. We wis tryin' tae get him to come out of the midden. He widnae listen tae us. We telt him no tae dae it.'

We follow her back into the midden, where she struggles to right the fallen bin. Joe is smiling: he is watching a pigeon pick its way between shards of glass on the back-court wall.

'Joe's comin' in for his tea, now,' she tells us, grabbing his sleeve and leading him towards the back close.

'See?' I say to Doreen. 'I telt ye Joe's mammy never gets cross wi' 'im. It's because he's a poor soul.'

On Mondays, it's Mammy's turn to use the wash-house. She goes down early to light the coals under the boiler.

Later she carries down the big basket of dirty washing. It's heavy and she stops for breath on each landing. Mammy's glad that we live on the third floor, and not on the fourth like the Duggans and the McPhersons. I get to carry the washboard and the bar of thick yellow soap. Mammy scrubs and rubs, leaning over the big enamel sink. Mammy says we mustn't touch the mangle or we'll get flat fingers and have to go to the hospital and Mammy says some people never come out of there. When the sun shines, Mammy pegs out the wet things on the lines in the back green. Mammy says fresh air makes them smell nice. Towels flap above our heads in the breeze, and the sheets billow and whack, and the sounds echo back from the tall tenements.

Mammy doesn't mind if we play skipping while she's doing her washing. 'At least it keeps ye oot o' ma hair,' she tells me. I like Mammy's hair. It goes frizzy when her headscarf slips off in the wash-house.

'Ye could put it through the mangle, Mammy.'

Mammy just shakes her head.

We can't skip on Tuesdays. It's Mrs McWhirter's turn for the wash-house, and she chases us off.

'Just you keep that dirty rope away from my whites! An' no balls, either!' she says. 'Ah'll be watchin' ye!'

We watch her from the entrance to the back close. Each time she comes out to peg up more washing she glares in our direction.

We climb the stairs, two at a time, to the fourth-floor landing and chap on the shiny white door.

'Mrs Duggan, is Joe comin' out to play wi' us today?'

'Aye, then I'll get my ironin' done.'

Joe comes to the door. Mrs Duggan pulls a blue jumper over his head and slips his unresisting arms into the sleeves.

His eyes are the same colour as the jumper and they twinkle as he smiles at us.

Slowly, we coax Joe down the stairs, waiting for him on each landing.

'We'll do skippin' today, Joe,' we tell him and show him the rope.

We reach the back green and hear Mrs McWhirter in the wash-house singing 'Mhari's Wedding' at the top of her lungs. We had forgotten it was her washing day. I grimace at Doreen and she laughs.

We leave Joe at the back close, creep towards the wash-house and peer round the doorway. Mrs McWhirter is bent over the sink, head shrouded in steam, sleeves rolled up beyond her elbows. Her stripy skirt strains across her fat backside and I point to a zigzag of stitches where the seam is splitting. Doreen holds her hand over her mouth so she doesn't giggle.

' "Step we gaily, on we go, heel for heel and toe for toe . . ." ' Mrs McWhirter's movements mark time with the steady rhythm of the song as she rubs the wet washing up and down against the tin washboard. Her hands look red and sore, just like Mammy's.

We tire of playing shops and houses. We pick dandelions, carefully, so as not to damage the soft white-down heads, and we count the hours as we blow the seeds across the grass.

'One o'clock . . . . two o'clock . . .'

Joe likes this game, so we find a dandelion for him to blow too.

We sit, elbows on knees, on the back step. Joe copies us and we all laugh. The back green is filling up with washing. Long, regimented lines of sheets and pillowcases, standing to attention like Mammy's jam-jars. On the line closest to us are Mr McWhirter's blue overalls, his shirts, his long johns, Mrs McWhirter's striped dress, all looking like people with no arms and legs queuing for a tram and having a wee dance while they're waiting. And there – there, at the end of the line, are Mrs McWhirter's bloomers! A red pair and a white pair! The breeze inflates them; they become the sails of sailing ships, balloons in a fairground. Doreen and I exchange nervous glances and snigger, aware we are privy to a forbidden sight. Joe sniggers too, though he is looking at us, not at Mrs McWhirter's bloomers.

Mrs McWhirter finishes her washing, stomps towards us, pushes between us to enter the back close.

We want to play skipping. The washing flaps haughtily as though reminding us it has prior right to the back green. The end of the washing line is twisted around metal pegs at the top of the post. Joe is tall. Joe can reach the pegs. We take an arm each, lead him to the nearest post, point at the washing line. I twirl my hands around, miming unravelling the rope. Joe grins. He reaches out and takes the end of the line in his thick fingers; carefully, he begins to unwind it from the pegs. He looks to us for approval, and we nod and beam encouragement.

'Yes, Joe! That's the way!'

The line begins to loosen. There is a jolt and the washing sways and jerks as Joe catches up the slack. Overalls, shirts, dress, long johns, bloomers: for a second or two all are united in an eightsome reel. Then Joe lets go, the line unravels quickly and the washing sweeps low to the ground, as though it is taking a bow after its performance. We giggle nervously at the line of tangled clothing, reminiscent of the counters at the church-hall jumble sale. Joe steps forward and begins to pick up the nearest items from the grass. The thrill and the horror as we realise he is clutching Mrs McWhirter's bloomers! He waves them in the air, red and white flags. We cheer and Joe laughs.

Then, the angry squeal of a window opening. We look up. Mrs McWhirter's face is the colour of Mammy's hands on washdays. Joe grins up at her and waves his flags some more. Long moments pass as Mrs McWhirter thumps her way down to the back green, with an anxious Mrs Duggan in tow. Above us, tenement windows frame disapproving faces, eager to witness the outcome.

'We told Joe not to do it,' we lie. 'But he's bigger than us.'

Joe is still smiling, though less certainly now. He looks at me but I look away. I don't want to see his blue eyes right now. He begins to stroke a streak of mud from the cotton bloomers. Gently, like a caress. He does not realise he has been betrayed.

'Ah'll be huvin' ma unnerwear, if ye don't mind!' booms Mrs McWhirter, thrusting out her hand.

Joe holds out the offending garments towards her. She snatches them from him, stuffs them into the large pocket at the front of her pinny.

She vents her anger on Mrs Duggan. 'He should be locked up, that yin! He's no' safe to be allowed out. And ye canny expect them wee bairns to look efter 'im!'

Mrs Duggan mumbles apologies as both women busy themselves picking up the line of fallen washing.

'Ah'll rewash the clothes that are dirty,' Mrs Duggan volunteers. Her voice is thin and reedy.

But Mrs McWhirter grabs the pile from Mrs Duggan as though she might contaminate them, and throws them into her basket.

'Ah'll do that mysel'. You just get yon eejit away where he canny dae ony maer harm!' She marches towards the close.

Mrs Duggan addresses her retreating back. 'Ah'll do that, Mrs McWhirter. Ah'll fetch 'im away now.'

Mrs Duggan turns to Joe. She has bright-red patches on her cheeks and her eyes are watery. She has forgotten that we are there. We hang back against the wash-house wall as she puts an arm around Joe's waist and steers him towards the close. He turns his head towards us, but we look at the ground.

I kick my sandals hard against the wash-house wall.

'Well, Joe didny really get into trouble,' I reason. 'His mammy didny tell him off or nuffin'.'

Doreen nods her head firmly in agreement. 'Ye'r right an' a', Margaret. You 'n' me – we'd huv got skelpt if we'd done sumfin' like that.'

The Websters live across from us on the third floor. Mammy always sniffs when Mrs Webster's name is mentioned. She tells Mrs Duggan, 'That Mrs Webster's a stuck-up cow. An' the looks she gies ye! Ye'd think she was aye sookin' a sherbet lemon!'

Linda Webster tries to be our friend but we won't let her. She's a cry-baby. Her mammy comes out to tell us off if Linda so much as whimpers. 'Play nicely!' she tells us, jabbing a finger at me. 'You, Margaret Kerr, you should know better! Linda's no' as old as you!'

Mammy says Linda is a spoilt brat and Mrs Webster dresses her up like a china doll you'd keep on the mantelpiece. Her Uncle Billy works away on the ships and when he comes home he brings her presents from all over the world. Doreen and I especially like the doll with blue hair. And the big conch shell which you hold to your ear so you can hear the sea. That's the same sea that her Uncle Billy sails on.

We are sitting with Joe on the step at the back close. We have been skipping and we stop for a rest. My sandals are scuffed and I know Mammy will be cross. We hear a tip-tap-tip-tap echoing from the stairwell. It gets louder as Linda comes down to join us. She has been away visiting Uncle Billy. She is wearing a green dress and shiny black-patent shoes which gleam when she walks. She struts before us, then twirls so we can see her new petticoat.

'It has lots of layers,' she tells us, 'so ma dress will stick out.' As she twirls, a large, green-silk bow bobs on the side of her head. It looks a bit like the giant frog in one of her storybooks. I wonder if it might turn into a handsome prince and flatten her. I like the thought of someone sitting on Linda's head and squashing it.

Linda turns to Joe. 'Joe, do ye like ma new dress?' She makes another twirl just for him. We glimpse the creamy layers of lace beneath the green material.

Joe smiles at her.

'Ah huv a dolly wi' blue hair,' she tells him.

Joe beams, his eyes fixed on the bobbing ribbon.

'Joe's our friend, not yours,' I tell her. 'That's better than a dolly wi' blue hair.'

'Joe's ma friend tae.'

'He isny.' I shake my head emphatically. 'Joe does what we tell him,' I proclaim as proof of Joe's friendship.

'You're fibbin', Margaret Kerr. Show us, then!' Linda waits expectantly, arms folded across her chest, the green bow lying still against the side of her head as though it, too, is waiting for evidence. I want to snatch it off.

I order Joe to stop looking at Linda, but he doesn't understand. She laughs and gives another twirl. Another glimpse of the creamy petticoat. Suddenly I want to trample it in the dirt.

I turn to Joe. 'Joe.' I pinch his hand to get his attention. He smiles at me. 'Joe, get the petticoat!'

Doreen leans forwards and lifts the hem of the green dress. We both point to the spotless creamy folds.

Doreen gives a little tug and laughs. Joe likes it when we laugh. He leans forward, too, and grabs the petticoat in his large fist. Linda squeals and pulls away, running into the close. We all follow, enjoying the game. Linda's patent-leather shoes slap-tap frantically on the stairs, she slips, and Joe is upon her. He is grinning. He pushes up the green dress to get at the petticoat, grasps it firmly in both hands and tugs with all his might. There is the delicious, horrible sound of tearing cloth, replaced by Linda's shrieking as she writhes on the stone steps, dress over her head, knickers exposed. We shrink back.

The stairwell echoes to the sound of footsteps and urgent voices. Anxious faces appear over banisters on all floors and a battalion of floral pinnies descends on Joe. Linda is snatched up in a flurry of green and cream, her screams muffled as she is pressed against her mother's ample bosom. Joe clutches a remnant of lacy petticoat in both hands, backs down the stairs until he is pressed up against the white-tiled wall. The aproned commandos, helmeted in their tightly bound headscarves, move in. Joe crouches, outflanked; his arms cover his head. Like two Tommies in the safety of a shell-hole, Margaret and Doreen crouch by the side of the banisters and watch the action.

'Bastard!' The word is shot by a sniper to Joe's left.

The artillery opens fire.

'Pervert!'

'Rapist!'

'Weirdo!'

Joe cannot comprehend the words but the tones in which they are delivered pierce his soul. He moans with the pain of it.

The ranks part to allow through Mrs Duggan. Wordlessly, she pulls Joe to his feet, shields him with her arms as she ushers him through the narrow gap between the floral prints. Mother and son scurry up the stairs and away from the field of conflict.

'It a' comes out in the wash,' Margaret's mammy says to the neighbours, shaking her head wisely. They are huddled together in a colourful array of pinnies, exchanging opinions in affronted tones, plotting tactics, planning reprisals. Arms folded tightly beneath copious bosoms add emphasis to thin-lipped expressions of anger and disgust.

'Ah was aye sayin' that eejit should get committed,' Margaret's mammy says to her pa as she serves up mince and tatties that evening. 'Ah was never sure o' that yin. You never knew whit wis goin' on in that heid o' his, did ye? Should've been locked away long since.'

She clunks the pot back on the cooker ring.

'Now we can sleep safe in wir beds at night. It's a' for the best, that's whit Ah say.'

Mammy says it wasn't the flu that carried off Mrs Duggan that winter. She says that Mrs Duggan lost the will to live. It's all for the best. That's what Mammy says.

JO LLOYD

Because It Is Running By

THIS IS Edie, Wil, said his mother. She's going to be helping me out.

He frowned at the girl, with her pale skin and hair pulled back in a ponytail, and she looked right back at him, cool as you like.

When was this decided? he said.

I told you I was going to get some help.

Didn't think we'd settled on it, he said.

He remembered that there had been a conversation. We can't afford it, he had said.

The B&B's the only thing making money, his mother had said.

We just need the weather, he had said, the veg'll pick up.

I'm tired of it, she had said, morning noon and night, never a moment to call my own.

He had seen his mother stopping at her work, closing her eyes, seen her falling asleep in front of the telly in the evenings. He didn't know what she would do different if she had more time.

It's just for the summer, said his mother. While we're busy.

Edie's job was to do the cleaning, make up the rooms, help with the breakfast, let his mother talk.

The guests had breakfast in the room that used to be the family sitting room. There were still relics of its former

43

purpose in there, the dresser his mother thought was too good to bring into the kitchen, some old china she was proud of, a set of encyclopedias his father had spent a lot of money on, thinking Wil might find some clues about the world in there. These things had been pushed to the corners to make way for the breakfast tables. On each table was a vase of plastic flowers, next to what Wil's mother now called the condiments.

Wil had hardly been in that room since the B&B started. They lived in the kitchen now. He ate his breakfast there, sitting at the old table, eating the eggs and toast his mother gave him, watching Edie come in and out, fetching and carrying, telling his mother what people wanted, conveying comments and complaints in a matter-of-fact voice, as if she didn't know what the words meant. His mother stood over the cooker, red from the heat, wiping her face with a tea towel, taking orders, while Edie floated about in her wispy top.

Give me some of that bacon, will you, he said to Edie one morning.

She looked at him. Have you lost the use of your legs?

His mother brought him the bacon. You watch yourself, she said.

Edie was staying in the old caravan. When he was little they used to go on holiday in it, dragging it around with them like a piece of home they couldn't leave behind. They went to grey beaches where a bitter wind blew off the sea and the pebbles bruised his cold feet. In the evenings they sat outside the caravan in their jumpers, watching insects hit the lamp and die. The caravan had flowery thin curtains, he remembered, that didn't quite cover the windows. It trembled with the dreams of the people in it.

Edie was the first person to use it for years. When he was coming back from town at night, warm and hazy with beer, he looked across to where it stood, saw the light on, wondered what she did there every evening.

Edie liked the work. It required no thought and was hard enough to leave her tired. She did it a little better than it needed to be done. She cleaned behind things and under things. She polished the taps and mirrors until they shone. She smoothed the sheets down, tucked the corners, folded the blankets back gently.

Her work was over by the afternoon and then she was free. Sometimes, on her way out, she'd see Wil working in the field, planting, digging, stacking boxes of veg into the back of the old van. The summer was dry. The soil was starting to crack. Sometimes he'd be standing there, one foot on the fork, looking away into the distance, for minutes at a time.

She would take a book and go walking, along the river, up the hill, nearly as far as the sea sometimes. She would find herself a quiet place in the bracken, and lie there, the book unopened, breathing green bracken, gorse flowers, worm-turned earth, things pushing into life, things dying, things rotting down into the darkness. Insects busied themselves around her. Further away she could hear the sudden panic of lost lambs, the despondent bleat of those that had been lost a while. Further away still, the hum of cars heading for the coast.

In the evenings she kept to herself, refusing Mrs Parry's invitations to join them in the house. She would slice some bread and cut some cheese and wash some lettuce in the tiny kitchen that was next to the couch that was also the bed that was next to the shower. She liked the smallness

45

of the caravan, the few steps it took to go from beginning to end, the little space there was to accumulate things. Just what you needed and no more. Every morning she turned the bed into a couch, made it ready for the day, and every evening she turned it back into a bed. In the night she could hear creatures moving around outside, as if she wasn't there.

The river path passed in front of the caravan. One day, Wil, coming back that way at sunset, saw Edie sitting on the steps looking out over the river and the setting sun. The light caught her face, lit it up, as if a candle was burning beneath her skin.

She said nothing as he approached, watching him, smoking a roll-up.

Mind if I sit? he said.

It's your caravan, she said. The corners of her mouth curled very slightly. He had never seen her smile properly, he thought.

Not mine, he said, sitting.

She passed him the tobacco. Your family's, she said.

Yeah, he said. The family fortune. A caravan and a couple of muddy fields.

She watched him roll the cigarette. He was very careful and neat about it. His fingers were blunt. His nails were short and there was dirt under them. She looked away.

So you're from London, he said.

Yes.

I been there a few times, he said. With the school. And once with the boys. He didn't mention the once he'd taken Heulwen, thinking it would be romantic, and all she'd wanted to do was shop. It's bloody expensive, isn't it?

I suppose it is.

Never thought it was worth it. What's it got that you can't get somewhere else?

The sun had gone. The light softened, the slightest breeze rolling up off the river.

Mam says you dropped out of college, he said.

Sort of.

How come?

Oh, this and that, she said.

He waited. Right, he said. He looked at the river. You must've got good A levels then?

Yes.

What you get?

Good ones.

The cigarette had gone out. He relit it.

I could've done my A levels, he said. Could've gone to college.

Aha.

Left when I was sixteen. When my dad died.

She looked at him. How did he die?

Throat cancer. He held up the cigarette. Too many of these.

She nodded.

Least it stopped him talking. Nothing else would. He talked a lot of shit, my dad.

Yeah?

I always thought cancer would be slow, he said. A slow way to die. But it was really quick. We hardly had time to get his suit cleaned for the funeral.

Down on the river, birds were flying home, low over the water, with small fluting calls.

You got any beer?

She shook her head. Sorry.

He nodded, shrugged.

47

I was going to do business studies, he went on. Thought it'd help with this.

She looked where he gestured, at the fields behind.

Dunno if it would have, though. Only so much you can do with a spreadsheet, isn't there?

I suppose.

Anyway, I can pay people to do all that. Once things pick up.

Aha.

Makes more sense. I'll be too busy with the veg. Probably have to take on someone to help with that and all. He frowned, looking out across the darkening river valley, then he looked at her. So, you going to tell me how come you ended up here?

She smiled. Nope, she said.

He looked at her smile. You on the run from the FBI or something?

If I was, I probably wouldn't want to tell you about it.

You should smile more, he said.

Wil came to find Edie the next day while his mother was at the Cash and Carry. Edie was kneeling, cleaning toilets, wearing a nylon overall, a scarf tied around her hair.

That's a good look, he said, smirking.

She looked at him. Is that what you came to say?

No, he said, looking at the floor.

She kept looking at him.

Anyway, he said, some mates of mine are playing a gig in town. Want to come? As if it didn't matter what she said.

Sure, she said. As if it didn't matter.

What do you want? said Wil. He put his wallet out on the bar firmly, held it there, in front of her.

I'll have a Pernod, she said.

What?

Pernod. Her lips twitched.

Wil, said the barmaid. Hello. Nice to see you.

Bron, he said, looking over her head. Hello.

She glanced at Edie then back at him. Usual, is it?

And a Pernod for the lady, he said, still looking over her head.

Got that, have we? said the barmaid, turning. I don't remember it.

A space had been cleared for the band opposite the bar. There were four of them, and a double bass; there was hardly room for the customers. When they played, people sang along, clapped, cheered, laughed. Wil joined in. That's a good one! he called. Nice one, boys! He drank beer after beer.

After the first set he turned to Edie. Bloody good, aren't they.

Do you always drink like this? she said.

Like what? he said. Nothing wrong with having a few pints.

Do the girls like it?

What girls? He glanced over at the bar where Bron was pulling a pint, her cheeks pink with the rush. They don't mind. He looked at Edie. Don't you like beer then?

One of the band came past. Wil reached out. Hey, Geth, come here. This is Edie.

Geth looked down at her. 'Lo.

Hello, she said.

She's here with me, said Wil.

What did you think? said Geth, looking at her.

I liked it, she said. It's fun.

49

Yeah, it's a laugh, isn't it. He looked at Wil. All right, Wil?

Great, said Wil. Fucking excellent.

All right, mate. See you later. Geth clapped him on the back and moved on.

Must be nice to have somewhere like this, said Edie.

Like what?

Where people know you.

Yeah. Don't get this in London, I bet.

The second set was quieter, lilting, sad songs, the ukulele underneath like water running by on pebbles. She heard Wil start to hum along. He stopped when she looked at him.

In the narrow space between the band and the tables the usual people were dancing, old Dick Powell and his wife, in their Sunday clothes, waltzing carefully, a few underage kids, stupid on alcopops, holding each other up.

Do you want to dance? he said. He had been trying to say this for some time.

She shrugged. OK.

He got up. Then he hesitated. I'm not much of a dancer, he said.

She was already on her feet. It's just standing with your eyes closed, she said, looking amused.

With his hands on her waist, he could feel her skin through the thin shirt. For all her paleness she was warm, like the stored heat of the sun.

When he opened his eyes she was looking right at him.

They got a lift back from a friend of Wil's. This is Edie, said Wil, dragging a tall loose man towards her. She's with me.

The man nodded, looking at the ground. He didn't say a

word all the way. Wil insisted Edie sit in the front. He sat in the back, leaning forward between the seats, talking for all of them.

They walked down the lane in the dark.

Night then, she said, when they reached the turn-off for the caravan.

Wil looked at her. How about a coffee? Or a fag? Or something.

I've got to get up to do the breakfasts, she said. And I think you'll need your sleep.

Me? he said. I'm great. Never been better.

Good, she said.

I can hold my drink, he said.

Fine. Good. See you tomorrow then.

He watched her walk away into the darkness.

He started to come over to the caravan in the evenings. I got no money to go out, he would say.

OK, she would say. She thought it was probably true.

They would sit together, sharing her tobacco, watching the darkness fall.

Wish it would rain, he would say.

She had noticed that everything about the place was improvised, temporary. Patches of old carpet laid on the field, plastic sheeting propped up with coat hangers, gates tied with string. There was a broken window at the back of the kitchen with polythene taped over it.

We used to have all that, he told her, gesturing up towards the road. That field there, see, with the cows in it, my dad sold that to the estate. And those houses up there, across the road, that used to be our land once. My granddad's land.

She looked at where he was pointing.

Nothing left to sell now. He frowned. Or it'll be all gone. What then?

He looked at her.

His kisses were soft at the start, careful, and then less so.

Under his clothes, sharp lines divided the rough brown skin that had been out in all weathers from the white skin that had been kept covered.

Don't say anything to Mam, will you, he said.

Every evening he came round. He took his clothes off easily as a child. She saw, as if from a great distance away, how naked he was. As if he had no idea how to protect himself.

He was watching telly with his mother in the kitchen after tea. They were sharing her Benson & Hedges, the ashtray balanced between them where the arms of the chairs were squeezed together.

Bloody comedians, she said. Making fun of people.

It's just a laugh, Mam.

Like it's our fault. Like we said, Oh yes, I'll get old and sore, thanks very much. Now make fun of me.

He looked at her. She'd aged ten years when his father had died. Don't take it so serious, he said.

Wait till you get to my age, she said. You'll see what's serious.

All the more reason to have a bit of fun, he said.

She looked at him. You've changed your tune.

He ground his cigarette out. Dunno why you say that.

She looked back at the television, the credits rolling too fast to read. You know Edie'll be leaving next week, she said.

What?

52

Schools go back soon. Only a few bookings after this.

You can't chuck her out.

Don't start with me. You knew it was just for the summer.

It still is summer.

It's not like she wants to stay. She's got it all planned.

Where's she going then?

You'll have to ask her.

She lit another cigarette, eyes on the screen. Not the bloody news. Turn it over, Wil. There must be something more cheerful on.

He didn't go over to the caravan that evening, or the next.

Edie came to him where he was in the field, leaning on the van. Come for a walk, she said.

He looked at the rows of beans going past picking, the seedlings waiting to be planted out. He looked at her. All right, he said.

They took the river path. The sun was fiercer than ever, as if it had to spend all its heat before winter came. In the middle of the river, where logs and shopping trolleys had lodged into temporary islands, cormorants held their wings wide, their throats to the sun.

You knew I'd be leaving, she said.

Course, he said, shrugging.

They climbed the hill over the river and sat, looking down at the valley, the bracken tall around them.

Where you going then? he said.

I'm thinking about Marrakesh, she said.

Marrakesh!

Yes. Morocco.

I know where bloody Marrakesh is, he said.

Have you been there?

You're joking, aren't you. I never been abroad.

Really? Not once?

Never been abroad. Never been on an aeroplane. I'm just a fucking peasant.

Don't do that, she said.

I seen you thinking it, he said. With your Pernod and your fancy accent.

That's not what I think.

What, then?

She sighed, lay on her back, looking up at the sky. I think you are where you are.

What does that mean?

I don't know. It's a good thing.

They were silent for a minute. Wil pulled the curled end of a bracken frond through his fingers.

So you reckon you'll be safe from the FBI in Morocco?

Turns out they're everywhere, she said.

He looked at her. Her pale skin and the curve of her mouth. He thought of Heulwen on the train back from London, the warm weight of her sleeping against his shoulder, of kissing her in bus shelters and phone boxes and the back seats of buses, of Lisa in the pub, laughing at everything he said, her hand climbing his leg, of Jackie, of Bron, of girls whose names he couldn't even remember, all their cheerful open faces, all of them the same, he saw now, just the same, too cheerful, too open.

He looked at the river running by down below. I had this mate Rob, he said. In school. Used to get this dope that was supposed to be from Morocco. Good stuff it was. Moroccan black.

She smiled.

But I don't think he's ever been further than Cardiff.

It was the time in the afternoon when everything stopped moving. The gulls went down on to the river. Buzzards drifted away into the distance like shreds of cloud.

He got married, Wil said. Had a kid. Then he turned his car over. He was in a coma for three months. I don't know. He's not the same. Everything's like a surprise to him now.

She looked up at him.

He's there with his family, just like always, kid on his knee. Loves that kid. And he's always smiling. Happiest person I know. But nothing's joined up. Just bits floating about.

She kept looking at him, shading her eyes with her hand.

I could go to Morocco, he said. There's no bloody law says I got to stay here.

He thought of the lettuces that he'd cut that morning, the cleanness of them, the cool outer leaves and the heart folded tight in on itself, of the way the land sloped down towards the river, the herons flying over, slow and wounded, to drop into the water, his father crumbling the soil between his fingers, the dark hollows where the sun never reached.

He lay down beside her and buried his face in her neck. She smelled of soap and gorse flowers, of sunlight and bracken and earth, things living, things dying, things continuing in the same way.

JANNA CONNERTON

The Stripper and the Dead Man

THE YOUNG woman supposes she has arrived at her destination. She looks up to the summit of the tower block and back down again. The dirty windows detail the theatrical ordinariness of life, every one a stage debuting a new tragedy or comedy each day. She looks again at the folded piece of paper in her hand and presses a buzzer that is held together with cobwebs. The old woman answers and permits her entry to the block. One flight of stairs takes her to flat number 17. The old woman opens the front door and nods as if to say, You can come in but don't expect me to have a party or be happy about it.

The young woman steps inside and is met with the dry heat of the desert; she removes her coat and reveals that she is dressed as a nurse. At first she tries not to breathe lest she inhale particles of fossilised dust, or worse. She would panic but the musty spearmint of her chewing gum reassures her. She glances into the living room, the carpet the brown and cream swirls of her childhood. The curtains brown, pulled back just minutes ago. The flat a theatre in front of the world. The play commences.

The old woman picks up her shopping bag and heads to the door. She calls back as she goes.

57

'Goodbye, Crutch.'

The reply comes from the bedroom. 'So long, Fat-arse.'

She shuts the door behind her and sets off down the road not looking back.

The young woman moves in the direction of the voice. She finds an old man in a bed that has become his home.

The old woman turns the corner at the end of the road and crosses in front of a white van she doesn't see; the driver swerves and swears. She mounts the pavement and watches as the van disappears around the corner. Usually she would swear back; today it doesn't occur to her.

As she walks she thinks of the old man forever in bed and grows sad at the thought. But then she thinks of him differently and has to smile. Lately he has started to say such things as 'Look at the rack on that one' or 'I'd put my face in a pair of those and never come up for air' whenever a young woman appears on the television. He even says it when they have the grandchildren over so she supposes it weighs heavy on his mind. A man shouldn't go to the ground with something like that weighing heavy, she thinks. Heaven he ain't going to anyway.

The young woman enters the room slowly, taking her first real breath since entering the flat. The old man looks at her and makes a noise that sounds like 'Huh'.

'All right,' she replies.

She looks around the bedroom, takes in the aromas, and sits in the chair next to the bed. She perches on the edge and crosses her legs, minimising the contact of her body

58

with the fabric of the room. The chair is turned inwards slightly so that the occupant can see the old man. His skin lies slack on his face like gauze on a burn victim, his head unsure of its place on the shoulders. His shoulders are propped up by pillows but the pillows have slipped down and the old man has slipped with them. Now he is collapsed and looking at the wall, the opposite direction to the chair. The intimacy of the careful placing of the chair lost, it now appears that the old man is angry with his visitors, that they have affronted him in some way and he tries to escape from them.

The young woman thinks that if she knew him better she would rearrange his pillows but that is not what she is here for today.

'Name,' asks the old man to the wall but addressing the young woman.

'Electra,' replies the young woman to the side of the old man's head.

The old woman cuts through the back way in order to avoid other people and their tales of who is in hospital or who has died lately. She speeds up with her heartbeat and then remembers she is supposed to be taking her time. She counts her steps and looks at clouds.

'Electra. What kind of a name is that?' says the old man to the wall.

'Not the one my parents gave me,' says the young woman to the side of the old man's head, as she rolls her eyes to the ceiling.

'Mine's Crutch but that ain't the one my parents gave me neither. That's the one she gave me. And it suits me, don't you think?' He laughs at his joke and this in turn becomes a cough, not so much a cough but a digging up of the roots of death that are planted in his chest.

After some talk of the weather the young woman tires of speaking to the side of the old man's head; she feels uncomfortable, as if she doesn't exist. She decides upon the intimate deed of shifting his pillows. She will shower when she gets home.

'Come 'ere,' she says as she leans over him to pinch the corner of the pillowcase between her nails. As she does this her cleavage looms over him and he sees the tunnel and a white light tinged with red. She heaves him up and he is roused.

The old woman thinks of items she will buy and of her friend Kim who owns the shop. Kim always asks about the old woman's husband although they have never met.

In the past the conversations have gone like this:

'How husband, friend?'

'Husband same, friend.'

Or:

'How husband, friend?'

'Husband in hospital, friend.'

The old woman starts to worry as she thinks of today's conversation.

'How husband, friend?'

'Husband getting strip show, friend, from stripper I found. Her card was in a phone box, friend.'

She stops and considers taking her custom elsewhere for today, just for today, but old-fashioned loyalty controls her. And she would be a stranger in other shops.

The young woman puts on some music. The dusty, battered tape on the bedside table where the old woman said it would be. Dean Martin, the old man's favourite. The young woman turns her back and begins to unbutton her dress. She removes it with care but when she turns around again the old man is asleep with his mouth open, his head once again facing the wall, plotting his escape. She explores the flat as far as the kitchen and makes a cup of tea for herself and one for him. She takes clean mugs from the cupboard but washes them anyway. She adds plenty of sugar to the tea and finds Rich Tea biscuits in the cupboard. When the tea is ready she removes her chewing gum with sticky pink fingers. She prods the old man awake and they drink. They talk while they drink and discover that they were born within two streets of each other, not far from where they sit now, but the street names have changed since the old man knew them. They talk some more of names of people and names of roads and how both should change in order to show that the world moves on.

In the shop tins of steak-and-kidney pie sit alongside Korean-made instant noodles. The smell of bleach battles with the hard spice of soy and ginger.

The old woman walks to the counter. Kim is there as usual. They greet each other and the old woman requests a pack of Rizlas, for the old man, but her face shows something of the way she is feeling. Kim takes her into the back room, the family's own living room, for the first time ever. Boxes of produce are stacked on the floral-print carpet, bulk bags of crisps on the armchair. The old woman tells Kim the story.

'A stripper,' says Kim and then bursts out laughing, trying but unable to keep it in. 'He will love you for this. Very . . . enlightened of you.'

'Strange, you think?'

'Unusual.' She considers. 'But a very loving gesture. God will approve, a wife pleasing her husband.'

The old woman returns to the flat, walking faster than she should, and finds Electra at her husband's side reading to him from the paper. They have solved that day's crossword, working out the clues together.

The old woman is sad that they have performed this most intimate of acts together, more intimate than that for which Electra's services were obtained. She had prepared herself for the stripping, but is hurt by the crossword.

She calls Electra into the hallway.

'Did you do it?' she asks.

'Didn't want me to. He fell asleep. Twice.'

The old woman is pleased but still wishes the crossword was half her work. She will read to him tonight and they will talk about the war: it pulls them back together like a bungee cord.

The young woman leaves with money in her pocket, tea and biscuits in her gut. She goes home to shower. Tomorrow she will visit her parents, who still live in the house where she was born.

That night, as she undresses for bed, the old man looks at his wife's landscape full of imperfections perfected over time, painted beautifully by centuries of true artists. He looks with his eyes that don't really see any more but have an imagination that sees all that was and all that will be. His head falls to the side, to face the wall, and he has escaped at last.

*　　*　　*

The old woman stays at home the day after, and the day after that. The next day she goes to the shop, to buy food and to see Kim. She has missed the smell of the shop.

'How husband, friend?' asks Kim.

'Husband happy, friend.'

ESTHER FREUD

The Crossroads

LEILA WAS born the same year as the Naqba – the Palestinian catastrophe – three months before Israel's birth. Not long after, her family had joined the first wave of refugees, walking with their baby daughter and what possessions they could carry across the border into Lebanon. I'd heard of her – Leila Mamoun – had read one of her novels, an intoxicating love story set in Beirut during the civil war, but it wasn't until we stood together at the Bridge, waiting to cross from Jordan into the West Bank, that we actually spoke. 'I hope you are a patient person.' Leila smiled at me as I wrestled with my bag.

'I try to be,' I said, taking a deep breath.

We were travelling with a group of twenty – writers, poets, journalists and film-makers – to attend the first ever Palestine Literary Festival. I had only recently published my first book, although I'd had two short plays produced, and I felt inadequate and nervous. 'I don't know what I have to offer,' I'd worried all week before the trip, and my husband steadied me by asking what I had to gain.

Ahead of me, Donal Murphy, a softly spoken Irishman of great acclaim, handed his passport to a soldier – a girl, no older than eighteen, in an outsized military jacket. 'Are you carrying a gun?' she asked him and, warned as we had been that we must answer any question simply, and refrain on all accounts from jokes, he hesitated, and then told her, 'No.'

'Ahhh.' The girl's face softened at the sight of my Jewish grandmother's name. 'Ruth. So beautiful. You know what this means?'

'Yes,' I nodded.

'Friend,' we said together, and I took my passport back.

We were outside in the sunshine, drinking mint tea and Fanta, our luggage X-rayed, our forms stamped, when I noticed Leila wasn't with us. Leila, Iskandar, Aseel. Muhammad. In fact all the Arab members of our group were missing.

'Where are they?' Everyone stopped their talk and looked around.

The festival organiser, a pale woman with a phone pressed to her ear, put a finger to her lips. 'They're being questioned,' she mouthed. 'Hold on, I'm trying to get through to the British Consulate . . .' And she turned away.

It was five hours before they were released. 'What happened?' we clamoured, offering croissants and tepid cups of coffee.

'The same as always.' Iskandar frowned. His mother was Palestinian, his father Welsh. 'An opportunity to fuck us up. They ask the same questions over and over until you start thinking maybe you do have something to hide.'

Aseel raised her eyes to the sky. 'Just a reminder of what the people here go through every day.'

The door of the office slammed and the guards, guns and flak jackets dropping from their shoulders, lumbered off towards their cars.

'They're closing now, that's all.'

66

'You're free,' I smiled at Leila as I climbed on to the coach behind her, but she turned and looked at me, her tired eyes kind. 'I'm always free.'

We sat together as we travelled towards Jerusalem, staring out at the parched landscape, the scrap and dust of a Bedouin encampment, the incongruous smartness of a trail of new brick settlements lining the ridge above.

'So how did you start writing?' Leila asked me, and I told her how I'd always been writing, it was just that, until recently, none of my stories had made it into print.

'And you?' I asked her and she told me that she'd had such a desire to be a journalist that aged seventeen she decided to interview all the leading politicians of her country on the subject of first love.

'I started with the Minister of Defence as he seemed the most unlikely to . . . you know . . .' and she looked as mischievous now as she must have looked then. 'I tracked him down to the barber's where he was being shaved. He was a huge man, heavy and fat, but with a little moaning voice. "An interview," he complained. "I'm not talking to anyone."

'I told him I needed the money from the newspaper, to study. I was saving up to go to Egypt. He offered to give me the money himself. "No." I hung my head. That wasn't what I wanted.'

Even now there was such disappointment in her voice, such sing-song beauty, I knew he couldn't have withstood it.

'So then the Minister looked ashamed. He called me daughter. "I will give the interview. But it must be now." '

Leila's article was a sensation. It appeared on the front page of *Al-Anwar*, a national Lebanese paper, and beside the overflowing photograph of the Minister of Defence was a small portrait of Leila.

'Were you as pretty then as you are now?' I teased her, and sincere, her elfin face opening in a smile, she answered, 'Oh, much more so.'

We were staying that first night at the Ambassador Hotel in West Jerusalem, and after a brief half-hour to rest and change we went to a small theatre near the American Colony to read and talk. 'Thank you for remembering us.' Bodies pressed in all around, eyes full of gratitude, hands applauding. 'It's the isolation that's hardest to bear,' they told us, these professors, writers, publishers and academics. 'Thank you for not forgetting.'

The next day we travelled to Ramallah. I'd imagined it as a far-off town but in fact it was no distance at all, twenty minutes on a clear day, but with detours and checkpoints it took two hours. No one was complaining. Most of the people we'd met the night before could not travel at all. They needed passes to get from one area to the next, and even with a pass there was no guarantee they would ever get where they were going. That morning we had our first sighting of the Wall, a grey barricade of concrete, eight metres tall, the land around it broken into rocks. 'Three and a half billion pounds,' Leila told me. 'That is what it has cost so far, and all paid for by the Americans.' We also saw our first settler. A teenager in surfer shorts and golden ringlets striding down the street, a Kalashnikov swinging from his shoulder.

In Ramallah Leila asked if I would like to meet one of her old friends. A woman named Zahra, a writer of novels and poems. I left my luggage in my new room, and ran back down to be introduced.

Zahra was waiting in her car. 'Let's drive around,' she told us, 'then I can show you what is being done.'

Zahra drove out into the country along a rough track. On either side there was parched land dropping down into a valley. After only a few minutes the road came to an end.

'There are many roads now that we can no longer use. And the settlement' – we raised our eyes from the valley below us to where a gleaming city had spread over the next hill – 'they have their own road that leads straight through to Jerusalem, look, they have tunnelled through the mountain, so that they can come and go without even knowing that they are in the occupied territory, our territory. And our rubbish tip, you see down there, that is forbidden to us since last year, but if you ask where to take the rubbish nobody tells us. Nobody knows.'

She backed her car up and wheeled around and drove fast through the deserted streets, telling us how, the day before, she had been turned down once again at a checkpoint on her way to visit her mother. She'd waited three weeks for her pass, but a soldier, a child really on his national service, told her she could not go through.

'I know it's pointless to shout, but all the same I couldn't help myself. "My mother is expecting me. She's seventy-eight years old!" But he said nothing, just pushed my papers back to me through the grille.'

We drove on in silence. It was possible we'd driven past her mother's door that morning.

'Next time I won't tell her I'm coming, then she won't be so disappointed when I don't arrive.' We had reached another dead end, and seething, dangerous, Zahra swung her car around.

I was anxious not to be the one to say it, but we needed to get back. We were expected at the university at one.

Leila put a hand on her friend's shoulder. 'Thank you so

much for showing us these things,' she said, and quietly we drove back to our hotel.

Our students at the Birzeit University were young and full of hope. My small group had studied Shakespeare, Chekhov, Pinter. They were knowledgeable and passionate about the theatre. I encouraged them to follow their dreams, to keep writing and performing. One girl, in full hijab, told me that as a child she used to hide away in the bathroom and talk to the characters she'd made up. 'Write down what they say, these characters,' I told her. 'Don't let them disappear.'

Later, when their questions had subsided, I asked a question of my own. I wanted to know about the clothes they wore. Why did some of them wear headscarves, some cover up completely, others walk around in jeans and flimsy tops? Hanan told me her story. No one in her family had ever worn a headscarf. Her mother never did, and her grandmother, when she was young, dressed in miniskirts and all the latest fashions, but when Hanan was eleven she had a teacher who inspired her with words from the Koran and she began to cover her hair. Her family tried hard to put her off. It's just a phase, they told her, and they left her to grow out of it. But she didn't grow out of it, and within a few years Hanan's mother adopted a headscarf too, and then, on the death of her grandfather, her grandmother turned to religion. 'Why are you wearing jeans, you naughty girl?' she scolded, and Hanan had to remind her that, only a few years before, she'd disapproved of her headscarf.

I told Leila this story as we made our way to a meeting of writers who had assembled in our honour. An elderly professor welcomed us, and we were thanked once more for coming. 'Occupation means isolation,' he said, 'which is why we are so grateful that you've come. Especially with so many people from around the world gathering to celebrate Israel's sixty years.' We sat around a large room and introduced ourselves. The people were dignified and often very funny, describing how they had used words to keep themselves sane during the recent siege. One woman had published a book of stories she'd written with the children, unable to play outside for months on end. Another, an account of being cooped up with her mother-in-law, whose continued presence in her house made her consider forming a new political party – anything to end the situation, anything for peace in the Middle East.

But there was one woman, in a frenzy of grief and rage, who appealed to everyone present to protest against two new settlements that were being planned. There were only three weeks left before it was too late. The room remained silent. There were so many settlements now, visible on every hill, smart, red-roofed blocks, looking down on the bedraggled flat roofs of the Arabs. We were aware that, in the past, people had protested, tying themselves to bulldozers, losing their lives. The international community had intervened, declaring the theft of land to be illegal, but the work had still gone ahead. We hung our heads, resigned.

The next day on our way to Bethlehem we took a detour through Hebron. We had to pass through the Calandria checkpoint. One by one we took our luggage from the coach and headed along an alleyway towards a cluster of grey buildings. It was very quiet, only one small family ahead of us, the man bent over in obvious pain. He was supported by his son, a boy of six, while his wife, ashen, clutched their baby daughter. They squeezed through the metal turnstile, made their way to the booth, and then to our surprise they came stumbling back.

'What happened?' we asked. We could see now the man had a tube protruding from his stomach, and the tube was pulsing blood.

Whispers hissed along the queue.

'They're being refused entry.'

'Added security.'

'George Bush.'

The woman was crying, silent tears streaming down her cheeks, while the boy staggered under his father's weight.

'Surely that man shouldn't even be walking?' Donal Murphy fumed.

'True.' Iskandar had taken out an inhaler. 'But Arab vehicles aren't allowed to drive through from one area to the next, not even ambulances, not even in an emergency.' He took a long deep breath and gasped. 'Twelve women died in labour at these checkpoints last year.'

We watched as the family pushed their way back through the last turnstile and were gone.

Silent, sickened, I shuffled forward, pressing myself into the teeth of the revolving gate. If only I'd run after them and offered help. Who was I, that I'd stood and watched? And all the fantasies I'd had of myself as someone who was ready to stand up against cruelty, who'd placed herself inside a hundred novels and risked her life for what was right, drained away as I showed my papers at the bulletproof window, and watched as a boy with braces on his teeth waved me through.

We were still subdued when we arrived in Hebron, a ghost of a place, the centre shut down, the markets closed, the houses boarded up. Until recently it was a thriving city of nearly two hundred thousand people, but then, twenty years ago, one family of settlers had come from America and set up home opposite the mosque. Since then, others had joined them, from Russia and the US, and now, even though they still numbered less than four hundred, an army of Israeli soldiers had moved in to protect them. In Hebron, roads too had been taken out of public use, and the Palestinians who lived in the houses on these streets were obliged to climb to their apartments by ladders at the back. Old ladies, pregnant women, toddlers. The only people we saw as we wandered through the streets were a group of teenage settlers, jogging, rifles slung round their necks. Later, in the abandoned market, we met one Palestinian man, showing his young son the house where his family once lived.

By the time we arrived in Bethlehem it was almost night. Our hotel was on a hill and above it the stars that must have been the Christmas stars were beginning to shine through. We walked through Manger Square, past the crypt which had become a church, and, slipping away from the others, I stepped inside and lit a candle for my other grandmother, a Catholic, who would have been amazed to know that I was standing here at the very spot where two thousand and eight years ago Jesus had been born.

That evening there were many questions from the audience. Who will tell our story? Who will listen? And there was much discussion as to whether books could ever change the world. There was no mention of violence, of rocket attacks or suicide bombers, and no one in our group thought to bring it up in the face of so many patient, gentle people, Christian and Muslim, still hoping that, somehow, one day, justice would be done. No one mentioned the Wall either, and the next day I understood why. It was too painful, too present, snaking its way into the heart of the city, seizing land and buildings, cutting lemon and olive groves off from their owners.

The next morning as our coach lumbered out into the countryside our guide explained that this was the last remaining point at which the residents of Bethlehem could get out of the city. Soon the Wall would be finished and never again would they have a chance to step out into the fields. 'This is where we've always come to smell the spring,' he told us, and he pointed out the markers where the next section of the Wall was to be built. 'They are stealing our horizon.' He stared out at the ancient land. 'Our children will grow up without seeing the sun rise or set. The Wall will be their limit, not the stars.'

In Jerusalem there was one last afternoon. One last night before we set off again for Jordan. It seemed a lifetime since we were here before. Leila and I decided to be tourists. We linked arms and walked through the winding lanes of the old market, alive with riches and beauty, birdcages and incense, silks and nylon knickers. We meandered from stall to stall, admiring jewellery and spices, chatting and smiling with the stallholders as we let our fingers trail over the goods. 'Here, let's go this way.' Leila tugged my arm, and she led me down a sloping cobbled ramp and in through the doors of the Church of the Holy Sepulchre. Immediately before us was a slab of stone over which worshippers were bending. Lamps hung above it on gold chains. It was where Jesus had been laid when he was cut down from the cross, and where now Christians from around the world spread out their possessions to be blessed.

In the centre of the church was Jesus's tomb. You could enter it through a small door and a queue snaked round in expectation. 'Girls.' Iskandar crept up behind us. 'Let me be your guide,' and he led us back past the tomb and into the mouth of a cave where he said dead bodies were once left to be drained of blood. It was dark in there, one flickering candle illuminating a shallow well, but he pointed out the groove leading down into the bowels of the building along which the blood could flow away. 'Now,' he whispered, 'gay men come in here to have sex,' and he grinned when both Leila and I gasped disbelievingly.

The Church of the Holy Sepulchre was unlike any European church. The floor was earth, the shadows long and dusty, and, clinging to its sides like moss, were other smaller churches. We traipsed from one to the next, snaking along corridors, marvelling at the variations on a theme. Ethiopian, Armenian, Greek Orthodox, Syrian. Out in the main courtyard groups of Italian and French tourists were singing painful, stirring hymns as they moved around the courtyard, marking the stations of the cross.

I photographed three Ethiopian priests against a bright-green wooden door, and then took a picture of Leila and Iskandar, looking on bemused as a middle-aged man heaved a hired cross on to his shoulder. We were all in high spirits. Our tour was almost over and the solemnity and tension of a week ago had given way to jubilation. 'This is the original entrance to the building.' Iskandar led us down the shallow steps that plunged through darkness and then out into the busy market. From here there was nothing to mark the site, just a stall selling baklava, a tower of it, sweet drenched pastry dripping honey and nuts. But before I could buy any, Iskandar showed us into a tiny shop. The shop looked closed, the two Formica tables wiped clean, but once we were seated a man appeared and, given instructions, began to spread a circle of thin batter over a flat grill.

Soon we were eating parcels of fine pastry, filled with nuts and cheese. Thank you, we nodded in appreciation, and then for a moment we all three became shy. It was the first time we'd been parted from the rest of our group, the first time in a week we hadn't been following a rushed schedule of talks and readings, meals and tours, checkpoints and interrupted journeys as we'd travelled the short miles between one West Bank city and the next. 'Why don't we walk back to the hotel?' I suggested, spurred on by new-found freedom.

Iskandar gave us instructions. He had a list of things to buy for his mother. He would meet us at the theatre for our final talk. 'Go straight along this road,' he pointed, 'and, when you come to a crossroads, turn right and then you'll see a small street, leading uphill. The hotel is at the top.' We set off, momentarily changing our minds about walking when a bus pulled up beside us, but after five minutes, when it remained stationary at the same stop, we decided to get off. The driver called us over and insisted we take back our fare.

'So did you get to interview the other politicians?' I asked Leila, picking up where a week ago we'd broken off.

'Yes,' she smiled. 'I got them all, and each time, just like my poor Minister of Defence, they melted.'

We came to an intersection that could have been a crossroads. 'No,' we decided, and we carried on.

'The Minister of Finance was the most difficult,' she laughed. 'I had to pretend to be interested in all sorts of other things I knew nothing about, but eventually he gave in.'

It felt like a luxury to talk about the past and not the brutal, concrete, checkpoint present. We began discussing our own first loves, and from there moved on to our husbands. Leila had been married for almost forty years. I'd been married for two. 'I think this must be it.' We stopped and looked uphill. It was a crossroads but there was no sign of the hotel. We turned right anyway, too busy talking to bother with doubt. But within minutes we'd reached a dead end. On one side was a shabby block of flats, on the other a patch of barren grass, and beyond it the back of a red-brick building. 'Is that the hotel? It could be?'

We traipsed across the dry grass, following a ragged path that soon gave out. At the top was a fence, three sagging strings of barbed wire. I held one down for Leila and lifted the ends of her shawl so that they didn't catch. Still talking, she did the same for me. 'The strange thing is,' she was saying, 'that even after forty years the same things . . .' And we were surrounded by dogs. They closed in on us, from nowhere, their lips pulled back, their jaws frothing and hungry.

A moment later two men with guns were on us. 'What are you doing?' they shouted.

I tried to speak but my whole body was shaking.

'We're trying to get to our hotel.' Leila spoke gently. 'We thought . . .'

Now we were here it was clear this could never be a hotel. Israeli flags hung from poles and the windowless expanse of brick had the look of a prison.

'Passports!' the second soldier demanded and, as we scrabbled for them, the first one asked, 'Where were you born?'

'England,' I managed, and Leila, more quietly, 'Palestine.'

They scanned our passports and then Leila began, with all the charm she must have used on her ministers, 'We're so sorry. We really were just trying to get back to our hotel. We'll go back the way we came.' She turned and there it was, across a railway line, the Ambassador. So unmistakably ours.

'We saw you on the cameras,' the soldier replied gruffly. 'You're lucky we didn't shoot.'

Leila took my hand. 'Would you be very kind and walk back with us to the fence, we're a little afraid of your dogs.'

The soldiers paused while they considered this request. And then, as if in spite of themselves, the pack of disappointed dogs trailing at their heels, they walked us back to the barbed wire.

ERICA ROCCA

Something Small and Understood

I ALREADY KNOW the look on my mother's face as I show her the hole in the bottom of my shoe. I see her pale, can feel the punch knot of fear in her body rise up to her throat as if it's my own. But I didn't do anything, I say quickly and defensively, it just went like that. The shoes, my only pair, are clumpy and second-hand, with a permanent scuffed shine, jolly balloon red, and tinkling buckles, a tallow-coloured sole. A more active child is responsible for the damage; perhaps they had been in the habit of resting all their weight on that foot. Maybe they had stood, bored and lonely, scuffing circles against flagstones in a playground. I know I'm innocent, and that no, I couldn't remember when it had occurred. There was only the creeping feeling that my right foot, my favourite foot out of the two, was more vulnerable than usual.

Now I'm too afraid to look because I fear the hole will swallow me up in some way. I attribute magic to it, give it a good reason to be there, but I'm already cynical. It would lead downwards, anyhow, to tunnels and jeering, clacking skeletons, so I'm not going to look. What if I start to sink into that place beyond my shoe? People will start to notice because I'll be limping badly, with one leg halfway in the underworld, and then I'll have no choice except to put my other leg in and disappear. I couldn't do that in front of my father, because he would only blame my mother. Everything is always her fault or mine.

Whenever I get dressed or undressed, my eyes avoid the shoe. I know I'm walking on something dangerous; I'm a monitor of tedious catastrophe. My foot becomes chillier and soggier. Yet it's the fault of another child; I vindictively imagine her to be very fat. It isn't fair, I think. At seven years old, I find my patience can still be flaky. I've made my mind up to tell because some of the popular girls at school have noticed and laughed. A skipping game ruined as they sneered at me. My face became blank before them, my poker face; the one that I have when I slip from my body, from the outside in.

I went away from my friends, picked up a stone, drew a sun with a smile and round cheeks on the sparkling concrete in front of me, but I'm ashamed, a little ball of anger, when my mother takes my hand at home time.

What's the matter? she asks. Lifting my right leg up behind me, as if checking for gum or dog mess, I show her, hear her say, Oh what have you done? simultaneously; then I see her face, the look, and start to cry.

Don't tell your dad, she pleads. Don't cry at home. You can't. She hugs me.

My mother is younger than the others outside the school railings; she's too thin and coiled. She always laughs awkwardly in groups. It's like watching an alien copying humans. We walk together now and say nothing. As we get closer to our street, she's like a boxer ready to take the final fight of his career. It's all there in her stance, the tension in her jaw, her face. Past pretty houses, dream houses, to our own with the nice hedge.

We step through the heavy door of our home, into the light-dodging hallway. Our house is different from the rest.

I've often heard my grandmother compare it to a black hole. It swallows sound. It's swallowed us. Christmas decorations and birthdays can't thaw this place out. Has it always been like this, the quietness without peace? Over the fireplace, there's an ornament of a breezy shepherdess and it mocks the three of us. It doesn't belong here, not polished and intact, anyway.

My father is out, for now, so we plan and collude.

For as long as we can we'll play hide-the-shoes, OK?

My mother has already dismissed the idea of covering the hole with a bunched-up sock. It wouldn't work, she says to herself. He'll know, he'll know. It wouldn't work.

My father has a frenzy for cleanliness. As she wrings her reddening hands, my mother decides that, whenever I'm in the house, the shoes will be taken and placed at the bottom of my wardrobe. This is something he hates anyone to do. Shoes are dirty, he says, and to be left by the back door, always.

On the second night – a Friday evening – he looks at the descending line of footwear on the linoleum, and asks, Where are her red shoes?

I'm cleaning them, my mother replies, with a fluting tone.

Her husband quietly accepts this answer, but he hovers around her for a few seconds, suspicious, slow. He reminds me of an old gorilla I saw in a zoo last summer. Without much fuss I walk into the next room to laugh quietly. She's become necessarily cunning, and is good at it if she holds her nerve. He's losing his grip on us, because we've learnt that his reactions are the same whether we tell him the truth or not. Our small unit contains the germ of revolutions and coups. We are deviants for trying to survive; a pair of witches, he once called us.

I wander back into the kitchen, but keep the smile behind my lips as my father leaves. At the sink, my mother now peels vegetables, and gives me a glance from underneath her curled fringe. I go over to her and tap her bony hip with small marzipan hands.

Can I do something to help?

Yes, take the peelings, she says, and scoops a damp mix of cream and orange strips into my open-book palms. We can't believe our good fortune at holding off the dread for a while.

It's more difficult to conceal the hole when I wear the shoes. My spontaneity sometimes peeps through when my short legs are dangling outwards from the sofa. On Saturday morning, I dare to lift my foot high while my father sits opposite, reading a newspaper in his fat armchair. A flick of defiance. My poor mother sees me, rushes towards me so quickly her sandals slapslapslap her heels, and whisks me off into the kitchen to help with the weekend wash. She says nothing when we're alone together, but her actions are curt with reproach. She whispers that I should keep myself busy, and points to my footwear: Think on, she says.

Too small to do anything but watch, I pull out a chair to sit on by the sink. My feet point downwards balletically. It feels as if there's a bright, glowing cord from my head to my feet, which will stay taut and good as long as I remember.

The old twin tub is being pulled out from underneath a low shelf, with an industrial rumble. Rust is bubbling its way along the bottom of this machine, once the pride of someone else's kitchen. A basket, very much like the ones snake charmers use, is brought from under the stairs. All the week's washing is contained within: lights, coloureds, underwear, darks. The tub is next to the sink, and juddering alarmingly, filling up with water. The smell of Acdo soothes, the cartoon angel on the box is there to make sure everything is better. My mother places her hands on the machine, and she shakes with it, watching now as three white shirts bloat like blisters and sink under the water. Leaning over from the seat, I notice as a sleeve wraps itself around the churning centre of the washtub. I imagine the shirt talking, crying out, No, I don't want to be washed! in a gurgling voice as she frees it and pushes it down triumphantly into the growing suds.

A few more minutes and they are done, to be lifted out one at a time, steaming hot, and hand-wrung for the spin dryer. There's sweat on her upper lip; the heat makes her pores prickle and she wipes her face swiftly. I'm aware that my mother's hands are quite ugly, that her dainty, plain wedding ring always looks like it should belong to another person. When I touch tracing paper at school, I think of her hands. They are more beautiful, only beautiful, when she's working. Her palms are glowing pink, the winter-blush cheeks of a happy child. The water has made them softer, younger, plumped out the grooves of her fingers. Now the nails are translucent, like small sea creatures. The strong hands twist the fabric, and the bony knuckles jut out even more. She's an artist at washing clothes. Small jersey dresses, bright plain T-shirts, and a number of trousers are picked up next, uncoiled and dropped in one after the other, like a sleight-of-hand trick.

This wash, more masculine than the others, will last longer to be on the safe side. It's an anxious nine minutes. My mother's staring into the opaque water. The trousers are more subdued than the shirts. They behave impeccably, and let her rest for a while. Then she says something which makes me realise that she hasn't been resting.

83

We'll be going to church after, she says. There's something happening at the church near town; lots of people are going. No, your dad isn't. We'll walk. There's no change for a bus, that's why. I'll fix myself up and brush my hair after this.

She lowers her voice. Your feet will be OK, just put an extra pair of socks on. Don't make a fuss, it'll get us out. Better go upstairs now and put them on, and play for a bit. Quietly. It won't rain again; the clothes will be OK on the line.

I leave, worrying about the weather; we won't enjoy ourselves if the clothes are outside and it rains; we'll walk home sodden and miserable, and say nothing again the whole way, that's for sure. I don't think church is worth it. Still, we're going out. The idea of out-ness makes me giddy, which makes me anxious.

Will three pairs of socks be too much? No, let my feet be safe, even if the rest isn't. An extra two pairs rolled out, pulled up, ready. I sit on the bed, afraid that 'play' will upset things. I won't be playing with Barbie any more after today. I pick her up in her lying love-heart ball gown, and put her down again. My decision is to stop being pathetic, and to begin now.

The same hollow rumble comes up from the kitchen, and I jiggle my legs, kick them up and out as much as I want, bite my lower lip in nervous excitement. Soon they talk at each other.

Holy Joanna, and he says it like a scythe. I can hear the click of my mother's knees and ankles as she walks up the stairs.

Are you ready soon? Have you done all your socks?

Yes, I'm ready, and, I want to say, I don't need toys and dolls any more. Let my cousin have her doll's house back.

The floorboards creak in the bedroom and bathroom; water gurgles. The smell of warm spearmint and cheap hairspray wafts out across the landing. When can we leave, I think. I want to see how normal people behave. I have to pretend to be like them too, like you do.

I almost slip as we descend. The coats are on, although it's May. We crowd together in the box hallway, exchanging looks and the other familiar codes like spies. A thought comes into my head: What if this is an escape.

Where are we going, I mouth. Where are we going, really? I won't need to take much, now.

Church, she says again. Church. I'm still not sure: she's wearing her own poker face, smooth as plaster.

We're going. She aims the words around the corner, into silence.

The sky promises the best for today, she says, brushing hair from her eyes. Oh, your hands are like toast. We always practise talking when we're alone. I talk about poems, and tell jokes. One was told to me at school by a boy with a pierced ear. My giggles become rapid and breathless as I tell her. It's about a woman and a milkman, and chocolate biscuits. I may not have remembered it right, as she doesn't laugh, but furrows her brow; she's listening, but she's being too serious, so I stop.

It's warm to be wearing the coats now. Heat rises up within them after each footstep. Everything's bright and blowsy; there's a holy sheen on the flagstones, and the wind blows the steam coming up from the tarmac. Water and air, cleansing.

We walk along the main road into town, under the cherry blossoms. There's an odd number of them along this Victorian terrace. One, two, three. Has she come this way on purpose? I wonder. Has she been watching them from her once-a-week bus, marking the progress of their transformation? Why not church tomorrow, on a Sunday? Has she put them to one side, as a treat for herself, like the lake surrounded by mountains I once saw from a car window?

The trees fill our eyes. We have time for them. The newly fallen pink petals spot the pavement; the older ones are decaying and tea brown. With a kinetic move of her right arm, my mother reaches up, plucks some fresh blooms, and tucks them into her hair, then does the same for me. We stop below a heavy loaded branch, one that's bowed down, and she shakes it: petals and water delight us, shock us. The flowers fall from our heads.

She's choreographed a memory, but dared to improvise. At the home place, every thought and action is measured out. A sentence can be chewed over for three days or more. Utterances of the smallest things are reabsorbed: there's trouble if they surface through a glance. Two of us, at least, know we're in a mad play.

Without her husband, and me, my mother is still a young woman, noisy, like the girls who sometimes walk past our house in the evening. I'm aware now that a man is watching us. Look, I say to her. He must think we're mental. My mother does her strange laugh and I watch her as she gives him a glance, one I understand from songs and TV, heady with cocktails, neon, perfume, other disturbing, exciting things, the things you have to give up Barbie for. He walks to his work van from the front garden of the house. White window frames, wrapped in shiny, taut plastic, are propped up against a brick wall by a white door. He whistles a slow, twangy song as she walks past. Back there, the other sits and reads.

Today, she's youthful. One hand in mine, her thumb taps out a rhythm on my palm. Does that tickle? Ha! Yes! Stop,

stop! I point out a stunted apple tree with fume-cloaked fruit overhanging a garden wall. She picks one and takes a bite. Yuk, bitter, she tells me, and flings it into the gutter.

Which of us is the child, and are we normal yet? We're more like foreigners now, tourists, than aliens. Teach me to speak French, I ask as she watches the traffic lights.

Bonbon.

Cancan.

Oh là là!

We carry on, through a wet suburb. I nearly forget to stride over puddles formed by cracked and sunken paving slabs. My shoes are feeling tight against the socks. Down we go, through unfamiliar roads that I have no savvy for, by groups of children in sweaters and jeans who stand quiet, or loll their arms on the handlebars of their bikes as we walk near them: *strangers*. They hover and stare like meerkats. This place leads to the outskirts of town, and we're now on untramped grass, across the way from a teeming roundabout. We look odd. People aren't welcome here; the footpath is narrow and begrudging. We're coming up to it now, she's saying. The noise is behind us, and I listen to it fade.

There's a long green avenue that appears in front of us; that's the overwhelming colour. No sky can be seen. The woodland on either side has formed a giant grove above. High, dark sandstone walls separate the trees from the road and footpath. Halfway down, but getting closer, there's an opening, a driveway. Closer now, I see a building. It's ugly – an experiment of squares and rectangles in concrete, with long narrow slits for windows.

This is it here. Can you smell the lavender? There's tons of it, it covers everywhere. It spreads. Look. Pick a bit before someone sees.

I grab some plump heads, squeeze them, and place them in my pocket. I'll carry the fragrance back with me. There are cars parked about, but not many. Where are the people, the crowds?

We go through glass revolving doors. I walk on tiptoe as we pass through them, trying to see inside. There's a glimpse of bright wood, pageantry colours on the walls, then a soft blast of incense as we're released into the church. My mother slows down, then stops, as if she's seen a friend. Here, she says confidently, and we cross over from a dark carpet to a marble crisp floor.

We're in a room with more wood, a sort of chapel where the glass in the windows is orange, amber and red. Room of warmth and flames. My mother smiles at an elderly nun, who smiles down at me. The pews radiate outwards in a fan shape before an indoor grotto, in which stands a statue of the Virgin, behind a thick red rope. She's the only thing in the room, or appears to be.

My mother side-hops down the front pew and self-consciously kneels. I copy her, wondering.

Pray, she tells me.

What for? I ask innocently.

She looks across at the nun, who isn't beaming at me so much now, and laughs a little. Her light eyes reflect a honey colour. For good things to happen. People like us, she says, people like us are rewarded.

Well, I'm going to pray for my shoes. Fix these ones if you want, God, Mary. I don't mind. I do believe in you. I'm praying really hard, because I do believe in you.

Mother of God high up, her ghostly shape. A row of snaggle-tooth candles throws shadow and light in amongst the folds of her solid robes. The sunset-blue eyes are almost rolled back in their sockets, to the right, at the wooden ceiling. Her swoony face. There are just three lines in the palm of each outstretched hand. Life, head, heart. There are already dozens on mine. My mother's workhorse hands are together in a perfect steeple, pointing up, not outwards. The strange colouring of this room flares the concaves of her face; the cheekbones like bruises, the mushroom-coloured eyelids flickering, baby-bird tender. Then she smiles, and I think she's playing a game, being mischievous. I watch and wait for the punchline, but she begins to move her lips, to slowly whisper, Hail Mary. Then it becomes louder, her normal speaking voice, then louder. It nearly has the tone of a football chant, the suppressed cockiness of the losers' side. Is this the joke? I feel alone and afraid. She's gone, to some other place that I can't get to. I turn to the nun, and ask for help with a look. The nun lowers her eyes, and studies her own lazily clasped hands, a conjoined fist. Is that a sheepish glance over at us? I shuffle from knee to red knee and make a renewed effort to be Good.

Amen.

The word finally falls into the speckled light. Relief. After a few minutes of being very still, the stillness where all you are is a pulse, what I feel now is this: that everything out there has been pulled away, a retreating sea of clamour. We were under it all the time. It's been a while since we lived, my mother says, then, What are you thinking?

We stay here for hours. Nobody asks us what we're doing. The pleasure is that we don't have to do anything. We do nothing. I lie back on the bench, and perhaps doze a little. Sometimes I wake up in the morning and wonder what my name really is, as I catch my reflection in the mirror across the way from my bed. My mother is a human-shaped air pocket, a cast of herself. Does she still know her name, and, if not, when did she start to be unsure? I've begun to understand what it means to allow yourself to exist. We're not mad, after all. We apologise so much, say sorry without ever speaking, but what for? The two of us should take up more space. Walking behind him like shadows! Sometimes I'll run ahead. I think these things as I look up at the ceiling.

There's a cold moment when the two of us stop being and listen to the roof for rain, but it's only footsteps of people in another part of the church. We relax, though the familiar feeling of shock reminds us too much of why we're here. No other people are in this room: the nun wished us goodbye and take care as she left.

Did she get it wrong about the crowds?

What's supposed to be happening today? I ask.

She says boldly, I wanted to come here. It's good, isn't it?

Then she points out details and the rest of her surroundings in a funny way, as if she's just recovered from an illness.

These windows. I remember them building this place.

That Mary, she says, nodding her head towards the statue, in the same tone she uses when she's talking about people who are crazy, or full of themselves. Mary rolls her eyes in outrage. Then my mother grins properly, and puts her arms around me.

Talk to me.

Talk to me. It has so much clarity. I'm surprised by her words. It's all we've wanted to say.

Will it work, praying?

I think it has.

I prayed for shoes.

I know.

Can we stay here, if we tell them, or ask them?

Ask who? No, I wouldn't want to be in here on my own in the dark. No! It's nice *now*, in the sun.

I don't want to go back.

Yes . . . I'm sorry. She squeezes me tighter. I'm so sorry. I know.

Her voice is now like the breaking wail of a child trying to make sense of things. A tear lands on the sleeve of her faded coat, with the tiniest dull sound. I feel stronger for the moment, no more sadness. Not today, when it would sit so jagged with the fullness of the cherry blossoms. I bring her back to the pretty room. It's warm, I tell her, but she misunderstands, and says I can take my coat off for the trek home if I want. At some point we stand up, and our gladness slumps. The sensation doesn't last too long. Happiness is a state I've become suspicious of. It's there to come down from. It's too unstable, and too dependent on other things. It's Christmas and birthdays. Joy is different, more resilient, dwelling in whichever place you exist. I've a feeling you can carry it around, and it can stay untouched. I'll make sure everything is OK. Realising this makes me calm.

As the two of us go outside and prepare to revisit the places where our old selves have recently been, we feed on the fragrance of plant oils, walk back into spring illumination. A slow-bloom event after the happening. We stop, and breathe, deep, deeper.

HILARY PLEWS

Lily's Army

EVERY AFTERNOON the shutters were closed at Singapore House for the siesta. Cook stopped cooking, Amah put Lily to bed and disappeared but, best of all, Lily's mother was out of the way, felled by the shutters.

Lily was finally alone, commander-in-chief of the sleeping house. Her army – the dolls – were lined up in battle formation around the table and chair-legs and flat on their stomachs along the bottom of the wardrobe. Their lack of anything sensible to wear was camouflaged by the ribs of shuttered light which seeped into the room and dulled the bright colours of their dresses. No one had ever asked her if she liked dolls: she didn't. They reminded her of snakes with their rubbery skin and blank eyes. The dolls arrived with monotonous regularity after her mother's trips to Raffles Hotel for afternoon tea – a place visited far too often in Lily's view, since she was never invited. She didn't complain. To do so would have lit the angry volcano that smouldered inside her mother, and once she had devised a use for them the dolls were almost welcome.

There were plenty of enemies crouched in the shadows cast by Lily's rattan furniture, waiting to take the place of the enemy asleep in the other room, but in the striped light of the siesta, it was the airborne enemies who were more easily spotted. Lily knelt on her bed and dispatched some of these with scythe-like movements of her arms, as they drifted downwards in their parachutes of dust. But the mosquito net she had been told NEVER, EVER to touch on pain of a good hiding constrained her enthusiasm, and she was forced to leave most of the action to General Wavell of Far East Command. He was assisted by General Percival, whose stupid plaits she had only yesterday cut off, and by the daringly named General Yamashita. Lily reasoned that, whilst he was on the wrong side during the war, he must have been a good soldier to have won the battle for Singapore, and therefore she *would* have him as one of her generals. The troops were obedient. Hardly were the orders out of her mouth than a battalion had rushed to repair a breach in the supply lines under the wardrobe, or had hurled itself into the darkest of shadow pools that dotted the bedroom floor to bayonet whatever lurked within. The object of the battle was both unattainable and totally desirable: to keep the siesta going until her daddy came back. He was fighting the Communists in the rubber plantations of Malaya and was away more and more often. His safety depended on Lily's army fighting as long as it possibly could in the dim light of the siesta.

Amah was the only grown-up who understood that it was important to fold back Lily's land of shadows slowly, so that the child had time not to show her troops the disappointment she always felt when she saw their flowery dresses and peep-toed sandals in the unforgiving afternoon glare. Lily's mother did not belong in the world of the siesta. On Amah's day off she crashed open the shutters, kicked the troops out of her way and snapped at her daughter to get up. *Now*. The shadows fled. She had no time for them. She wore bright lemons and limes and painted her nails a fiery red that clashed with the backs of the mah-jong tiles she clicked across the card tables of Singapore. She drank flower-coloured cocktails out of glasses with long stalks and smoked a lot. Her face was perfectly white and smooth, and whenever Lily was permitted to accompany her mother to an engagement she noticed that men stared.

Sometimes Lily was allowed to watch her mother putting on her face in the morning. When she smoothed foundation over the two deep lines that ran across her forehead, Lily thought of monsoon rain transforming their cracked garden into a green jewel. *One for the British Army*, her mother once said, as the top line disappeared beneath the foundation, *and one for the Japs*, as the flow buried the second line. It wasn't often that Lily's mother joked with her so Lily giggled, but she stopped immediately when her mother's face closed like a fist in the mirror. After the foundation was applied, Lily lost interest. She disliked her mother's red lipstick because it often got stamped across her cheek and looked silly, and when her mother made eyelash fans with a black brush it seemed overdone and false. Lily knew that men, especially Major Carshalton, a frequent visitor, thought her mother was beautiful, but he couldn't really read her mother's made-up face without lines. Only she, Amah and Cook knew that, beneath the smooth white mask, her mother was so angry that she could explode at any moment and burn for ever, like the sun.

Her daddy came back from Malaya.

'Hirushala!' he said, as he threw her into the air and caught her. Lily asked what they would do when she got too big for that. He promised to think of something. Lily thanked the Army for their good work and sent Wavell and Percival home to England for a rest by dumping them at the back of her wardrobe. She thought it would be all right to send Yamashita to Japan and was arguing the point aloud when Amah slipped into her room. She made a shush sign and began talking in Cantonese; something she only did to communicate extreme seriousness.

'Give doll another name,' she said.

'Why, Amah?'

'Your mother will be very cross with both of us if she hears that name.'

'I won't tell her.'

'I know. But you talk out loud – she might hear you. *I* did.'

'Oh. But I need good generals.'

'Lily. There is no such thing as a good general.'

'If my daddy were a general he'd be good.'

'Your daddy is a good *man*. Quite different.'

Everything was more fun with her daddy around. She could actually sleep during the siesta. He would play hide-and-seek with her and push her past that place on the swing where she was always stuck. He would point out all the animals in the night sky – the Swan and the Scorpion, the Crane, the Eagle and her favourite, Pegasus. Her mother looked less like the beautiful Chained Princess, who also sparkled in the sky at night, and more like other girls' mothers, because his jokes cracked her white mask. The cracks revealed sun rays at the corners of her eyes and crescent moons on either side of her mouth. She stopped buying dolls.

The three of them picnicked under the flame tree in the garden. Her mother smoked whilst she squatted on the soles of her bare feet. Lily felt strangely proud of her. Only children, Chinese and Malay grown-ups could do that. Her Daddy said once he'd made Malaya safe he'd take them to the Cameron Highlands, and there they would enjoy the cool dark under the great forests of oak and laurel.

'Doesn't the sun shine in Malaya?' Lily asked.

'You know it does,' he replied. 'But the forest roof is so thick that only a few fingers of sun can get through, so underneath it's shadowy and dark. Slices of the dark turn into bats if you stay still for a long time.'

'Mummy's scared of the dark,' Lily said, not quite certain what she based this on, but knowing it to be true.

Her mother's eyes glinted. She screwed her cigarette into the ground.

'Mummy's not scared of the dark,' she said. 'She's scared of the Japs.'

'Geraldine.' Her father's tone was Morse code for *Danger!*

'She'll have to know sometime. Anyway, it's true.'

'What's true?' Lily asked.

'Put it this way.' Geraldine's eyes bored through her daughter. 'I'd rather slit your throat than have you marry one.'

'*Geraldine!* Stop it.'

Lily's mother jumped up and headed indoors.

When Lily judged her out of earshot she said, 'I'm *never* going to marry.'

'She doesn't mean it,' said her father. His eyes followed her mother's progress. 'Some Japs are good people.'

'Was General Yamashita good?'

'Lord, the things you ask. I suppose he was a good general.'

'Amah says there's no such thing as a good general.'

'Amah's Chinese.'

With this, her father patted her on the head and went

inside. Lily was disappointed. He should have answered her question.

'Let's go to Raffles for tea,' he said one afternoon after the siesta.

'Yes!' Lily yelled.

'No,' said her mother.

'But I've never been and you've –'

'No means NO. Amah!'

Amah appeared immediately, talking in Cantonese, as if to Cook in the kitchen behind her: *Quiet, little one. I'll take you to Pasirpangjang market instead.* 'Yes, Mrs Hazelburn?'

'Take her away until she's learned some manners. Sorry, darling, Raffles is such a bore these days.'

Her daddy usually got his way. Towards the end of his leave he did take her mother to Raffles. Thankfully no doll appeared afterwards, and Lily was almost glad she hadn't been invited, because it was obvious from the silence between them when they returned that something unpleasant had occurred. Her mother's normally white face had acquired a flush and her mouth reminded Lily of a cut. Amah and Cook swapped glances. Their employer was in one of those moods when the most innocent of *Yes, Mrs Hazelburns* could turn her intermittent criticism of their work into an all-out assault on their personal dignity. As for Lily, she knew when to stay in the kitchen. She shovelled chopsticks of boiled rice and chicken down her throat and only half listened to Amah and Cook nervously gossiping in Cantonese.

'You think he knows?' asked Cook.

Amah shrugged.

'Perhaps he's found out?'

'How? We're the only ones who know.'

'They all know . . . maybe a warning? He likes *you*.'

'Ai yaah! You want my job as well as yours?'

The next day her daddy took her to the Singapore Swimming Club whilst her mother attended one of her mah-jong coffee mornings. She dived off her daddy's shoulders and performed underwater roly-polys for him. As she steadied herself for another dive, she saw Major Carshalton drinking out of a long glass and waved at him. He didn't wave back. In fact when she surfaced he'd gone, but his drink was still there, unfinished, on the table.

They ate kedgeree under huge sampan-like umbrellas for their lunch, and despite lots of laughter, she knew something was wrong.

'Is it because you're going back to Malaya that you're sad?'

'No,' he said. 'Who says I'm sad?'

'I do. Is it because you don't want to leave me and Mummy behind?'

'You know I don't,' he said.

'Do you have to go? I don't want you to go either. Don't go, Daddy. Daddy . . .?'

Lily found herself weeping uncontrollably. She longed to explain what a relief it was to have him home so that the dolls could be left where she had hurled them in the wardrobe; so that she didn't have to keep watch for him every siesta because she knew he was safe. He lifted her on to his knee and said that when you grew up you sometimes had to do things you didn't like, and that things happened you didn't intend, but that she was to dry her eyes, because otherwise she wouldn't be able to see the enormous Knickerbocker Glory he had ordered for her.

After her daddy's return to Malaya, another doll arrived

courtesy of her mother's trips to Raffles Hotel. This doll was even worse than usual and Lily blamed Major Carshalton. It was a feeble, stick-like creature called Una Señora de España with a long skirt made from layer upon layer of scarlet frills edged with lace. A black veil flounced its way down her back and was stuck to her head with a ridiculous comb. Lily didn't need any more troops and even if she had, this frilly *thing* was totally wrong. Despite the gloom of the siesta there was no possibility of that fiery, enormous skirt assuming, even in her imagination, the straight and sober lines of battledress. In the safety of her room she jumped on top of the doll several times before throwing the pieces under her bed. All armies lost troops.

Amah found the crushed body parts of the doll and squatted on the floor. She shook her head.

'We won't get into trouble,' Lily whispered. 'She never asks what I do with them. I'm going to tell her I don't want any more. In fact I don't need any now that I've got Yamashita.'

'I thought you were going to change that name?' said Amah.

'No,' said Lily.

Amah took a big breath. 'You know that when General Yamashita captured Singapore he took many English prisoners?'

'Yes. He put them in Changi. Everyone knows that.'

'And you know that he treated all of us who lived here very badly, but especially the English prisoners?'

'Ye-es,' said Lily, less certainly.

'Your mother and Cook and I . . . we survived General Yamashita's occupation . . . it is not nice to remind us of it.'

'No. No, of *course* not.' Lily felt that Amah had taken her to the edge of a cliff, allowed her to lean over for a second before pulling her back to solid ground. She would rename the doll Monty. She didn't think he had been in the Far East, but maybe that didn't matter.

One afternoon Amah rushed into Lily's room in the middle of the siesta. She disrupted Monty's march to rescue Percival's troops, who were lost in the deep shadows of the Cameron Highlands, and included her daddy. Her teddy bear's outstretched arms represented the huge guns of Singapore that were meant to protect everyone from the Japanese, except that they had been facing the wrong way, but not any more. On Lily's watch, she carefully moved teddy's arms to track her daddy's movements and keep him safe.

'Lily, Lily, you must get up now. We have to see your mother. Quick, little one, we have to be very quick.'

Everything about Amah communicated urgency. Her voice – breathless and high, the use of Cantonese, the fact that she tried to help Lily dress, even though Lily was too old to need help with this any more. When they reached the top of the stairs, Amah took Lily's hand. She kept a firm hold of it as they walked into the living room. Lily's mother was standing by the half-opened shutters, her back to the room. She faced them as they entered and Lily gasped. Her mother, caught between the shutters, was silhouetted by white-hot afternoon light and appeared to be burning up like a shooting star. Her scarlet lips shook and her long nails waved blood as she fanned herself with an envelope. She could hardly look at her daughter.

'Your father won't be coming home tomorrow,' she said. Her voice grated like the sound of mah-jong tiles being shuffled.

Behind the curve of her hand, Amah whispered not to say anything. Her other hand squeezed Lily's.

'Or at all. He's dead. Killed in an ambush.'

Amah let her hand drop as she repositioned herself behind Lily and pulled her close.

'Darling.' Her mother hardly ever called her that. 'I have to go out; there are a lot of things to do. Amah will look after you.' She left the room. The glare from her orange skirt swirled after her.

Lily sank down to the floor and squatted there, dry-eyed, her head between her knees. Not even Amah's hands on her back could save her from this cliff edge. She didn't know when she would fall, but she knew that when she did it would be alone.

Her mother said it would be too upsetting for Lily to attend the funeral or the burial at Kranji. It was left to Amah to tell her how straight the soldiers stood for their final salute, and how gently they carried her daddy's coffin on their shoulders. Lily's mother said she could attend the reception afterwards, as long as Amah kept her out of the way.

Lily thought her mother suited black. It showed off her white skin. She wore a small hat with a veil that just covered her eyes, below which her lips shone. Lily supposed her mother wore the veil to hide her tears. Major Carshalton divided his time between guarding her mother and pacing the room to talk to guests. He even came and spoke to Amah.

'How is she, Amah?' he asked, as if Lily was in another room.

'OK. Thank you, Major Carshalton.' Amah frowned.

No one else spoke to them, although some of the women smiled in their direction, without making eye contact. After standing in the corner of the room for ages, not knowing what to do and quite unable to eat or drink, Lily asked if she could leave.

Once home, Lily marched upstairs and dragged the dolls together in the fading light. Her daddy was dead because they had failed. She delivered several sharp kicks to her army and scattered them across the floor. She plucked Wavell, Percival and Monty from the mess. It took all her strength to wrench off their heads. The exertion produced rasping sobs and she fell on to the floor to lie amongst her battered and headless troops. She cried for a long time before she realised that punishing the generals would not lighten the ton of loneliness and guilt that now encased her like an iron lung. She, after all, was her generals' general.

There was one thing she had to do before either Amah came upstairs or her mother returned to chase away the quiet dark. She checked the night sky as her daddy had taught her. She looked along the lines of the Water Snake, through the Crane's trailed legs, past the Eagle to the soaring wings of Pegasus, the sky horse. Now she had North and could face Kranji Cemetery, and beyond that, Malaya. She stood up straight and saluted.

CHERISE SAYWELL

The Candle Garden

*P*RIVATE GROUNDS, the sign said. It didn't say *Keep Out*.
The gate was open and straight away Laura could
see this garden was perfect. Although a high stone wall
enclosed it there were no signs of any security, and in the
centre was a freshly dug bed. She stepped inside and stood
on the path for a moment, waiting to see what would
happen, but no one appeared.

'Come on, Connie,' she said.

As soon as she was inside Connie skipped ahead, flitting
along the fence to where a chestnut tree stood. Laura's
heart raced as she disappeared but she didn't go after
her. She'll come back, she told herself. She'll be looking
for conkers. There were a couple of chestnut trees in the
Botanic Gardens and occasionally you saw one arched
over the wall of a private garden like this. It was illegal to
touch, even if the branches hung right in your path.

Laura knelt before the flowerbed, smoothing her hands
across the loose soil. It was strange, that sign, because
the owners of a garden like this didn't need to state the
obvious. A high fence with a twist of barbed wire and an
intercom was what normally did the job. Outside these
guarded green spaces there were no longer any verges or
parks or drying greens. Everything was leased and fenced.
Even cemeteries were gated and secured. You could only

visit to inter the ashes of a family member, when they gave you a ticket to sit among the gravestones and the flowers for an hour or so. Apart from that the only garden for ordinary people like Laura was the Botanic Gardens where you paid and then kept to the path. For most it was enough just to look – to see the green of the untouched lawn, the bright strain of colour in the flowerbeds.

The last time Laura was at the Botanic Gardens the path was crowded with people: teenagers roaming in packs, workers enjoying a glimpse of brightness on their way home. It was October but still warm and thick as a summer's day. People had stared as Laura veered off the path and on to the grass, crouching to unpack her bag. Trowel. Fork. Bulbs like charred onions that she'd bought on the black market. Although the grass was mown close and tight it was easy enough to lift it with the trowel, and Laura pictured the buttery glow of her daffodils there. But she was uncertain of how deep to dig – she hadn't got this far before. She made several holes of different depths and placed a couple of her bulbs in them to see. It would be important to leave enough room. Connie had stayed close by that day, not saying anything, not even when the environmental warden came up to ask what the hell Laura was doing. A policeman was called when she kept on digging even after a crowd gathered to watch. Luckily no one saw inside her bag.

That was her second attempt, that day in the Botanic Gardens. Laura tried not to think of it now. They'd been quite lenient so far. They'd taken her home and given her a dispensation but that last time she had to take unpaid leave to make it stick. Now she had to light candles at night to save her power coupons. Each soft flame reminded her. She didn't tell anyone where she was going today. She certainly couldn't say she was taking Connie.

Laura reassured herself. She wasn't thinking straight those other times. Today she would do it properly. She thought of the unlocked gate, the sign, and smiled. It should have read *Private Grounds, but Do Come In.* Or *Private Grounds, Please Enjoy.* Beyond the shrubbery was a large house with tall glass windows and enclosed balconies. The roof sloped steeply and there were drains running off all the visible edges where the rainwater would be harvested and cleaned. There was also a well, sheltered, with a complex filter system arranged around it. The people who owned this garden would be very rich. They would not have to worry about when the rain went away. They could clean and store their water. They could bathe and wash their clothes and grow flowers. The thought of her proximity to all this wealth sent a quick jolt of panic along Laura's spine, but she reasoned with herself. This place wasn't manicured like the tightly fenced gardens of the gated communities further along the road. The shrubbery around the walls seemed untouched and Laura was able to identify a large oak tree and an unkempt aspen in the far corner. They lent an air of privacy, of seclusion, to the place. The border of the bed was not well marked but it was clear it had been prepared for planting. And anyone with a garden like this would want flowers.

Laura took a breath. There were four wooden benches dotted about the lawn. They had an abandoned look and Laura felt encouraged. She would work quickly and unobtrusively. She would finish this today. She pushed her trowel into the dirt of the empty flowerbed, turned the earth a few times and began to dig.

Nearly half an hour passed before Laura was disturbed.

'Are you the gardener?'

Before Laura stood a woman, tall and solid-looking, old but not frail.

'Pardon?' Laura said.

'Are you the gardener, then? The agency said they'd send someone today.'

Laura thought quickly. If she were reported now there would definitely be a fine, or worse. There certainly wouldn't be another chance. She sat back in a kneeling position and checked her clothes. Canvas trousers. Green pullover. She wondered if they would pass for a uniform.

'Yes,' she said. 'Yes, I am.'

The old woman narrowed her eyes, but only slightly. 'When did you start?' she asked.

'Today. Just now.'

'Funny time to start. Quarter after the hour. Middle of the afternoon. I opened the gate at lunchtime.'

'I went to the wrong place. I'm sorry. I'm a bit late.'

The woman sniffed but she didn't question Laura any further. 'Well, it's not before time, anyway,' she said. 'Useless, that last one. Dug up my peonies. Moved them.'

Peonies. Peonies. Laura only knew the names of a few flowers, mostly the ones you could see from the path in the Botanic Gardens, and some from the *Encyclopedia of Gardening* that had belonged to her grandmother. Flowers were currency if you were as wealthy as this woman. She was jabbing her finger in the direction of some foliage near the steps and Laura tried to look as if she knew the plant in question.

'They don't like to be moved, peonies,' the old woman said. 'But I expect you knew that.' She eyed Laura as she rested against her stick. It punctured the soft damp ground. 'Now they won't flower for God knows how long.'

'Oh. Sorry.'

'What are you sorry for? You didn't do it.'

Laura pushed at her cuticles. Her nails were dry and caked with dirt.

'Well, never mind,' the old woman said. 'It's just a matter of waiting.' She looked at the sky. 'Always a matter of waiting these days. Nothing happens when it should.'

Laura stooped and put her trowel down beside the bag, then scanned the back wall of the garden. Where was Connie?

The old woman followed her gaze.

'What're you looking at? There's nothing along there to worry about.' She huffed impatiently. 'I don't want anything done down there. Didn't the agency tell you? It's only these beds here I want planted. I don't care what with, whatever they sent along with you.'

'It's OK,' Laura said. 'They told me all that.'

'There were dahlias in there last year, chrysanthemums and asters. There were primulas around the edge too. It was a bit much really. A bit tasteless if you ask me. But if you can get them you've got to put them in, haven't you? So dry, it was. There was nothing off the roof for months. I had to keep the well water for the house. Those flowers didn't have a hope.'

Laura clicked her tongue, trying to sound sympathetic. 'Yes,' she said. 'It was very dry. Much too long to go without water.' She paused and then, unable to contain her irritation, said, 'We had to use the community well. I had to boil the water for my daughter to drink and she still got sick.'

The woman was staring at the well. Now she looked at Laura.

'Yes. Hmmm,' she muttered. 'Anyway, there's no shortage now. I've had them in to clear the filters three times already. Never mind. So long as you get something in that'll stay alive I don't care.'

Laura put her hand on the bulbs. Despite her annoyance she was pleased with herself. She couldn't believe her luck, couldn't believe the clever story that had knitted itself around her. And so far no other gardener had turned up. Now if only the woman would go and let her get on with it. She hunched over the flowerbed, concentrating. *Go away, go away*. If she thought it hard enough, perhaps it would happen.

But it didn't. The old woman waited a minute or so, then struck out for a nearby bench.

'I'll have a sit down,' she called back. 'I'll have a look at what you're doing.' She poked at the dirt on her shoes with her stick. 'That last one . . .' Tutting, she leaned her head in the direction of the wronged peonies. 'That's not going to happen again. I can tell you that now.'

The flowerbed was oval-shaped and slowly Laura worked her way around its perimeter. It would have made more sense to start in the middle, but she wanted to be alone when she did that. Briefly, the sun shone overhead before it began to weave in and out of the encroaching clouds. Laura planted the whole border before the old woman called out.

'You'd have been better starting there,' she said. She was using her stick to point to the centre of the patch and, even though she had been expecting a comment, Laura was cross.

'It's all right,' she said testily. 'I'm leaving a little avenue.' She indicated the narrow path of unsown soil leading out from the centre to the edge of the bed. 'I'm going to plant that bit when I'm finished. It's just that I want to do something special in the middle.' She checked the back wall again, where the chestnut tree was. There was still no sign of Connie. 'Does that wall go right round?' Laura asked.

'Yes. Didn't you see a picture at the agency?'

Laura could have swallowed her tongue. 'Oh yes,' she said, 'but I didn't look properly.' She thought quickly. 'They said I'd only have to do this bit so I didn't go over the plans.' The old woman was checking her over now, checking the trowel, the bulbs. Making sure. 'Then, when I got here,' Laura continued, 'I didn't want to intrude. I thought I should just get on with it.' She paused and then decided to throw in a little honesty for good measure. 'To be perfectly truthful, I was surprised the gate was open. I expected to be buzzed in.'

The old woman sighed. 'I'd rather spend my money on the garden.' She jabbed her stick at the ground. 'Anyway, I generally find it's enough to keep the gate closed.'

Laura felt the heat rise in her neck. She bent forward again, and began digging an inside circle, placing the bulbs as closely as she could.

'Is it crocuses?' the old woman called. 'You're crowding them a bit, aren't you?'

'It's daffodils.'

'Still a bit close.'

'Well, you've paid so I don't want to waste them.' Laura looked carefully away. She knew how she wanted the garden to look. She'd counted out the bulbs left over from the time in the Botanic Gardens and distributed them in her head, imagining the petals thickening to a smooth brilliant centre, like a flame. She hunched her shoulders and bent her body over the soil as if to ward off any further questions. But the old woman huffed and Laura sighed and looked up again.

'There's quite a few daffodils in this garden, you know,' the old woman persisted. She pointed. 'Over there, near the aspen, and in the shrubbery by the front path. Most of them dried out last year but I managed to hold on to a few. It might be nice to have a bit of variety in that bed.'

'Well, I'm sorry but no one has anything else,' Laura snapped. It made her angry, this woman who could pick and choose, even while she said she didn't care. But she softened her tone then, remembering herself. 'This was all they could give me.'

That much was true. There was so little to be had. Apart from the black market, you could only get plants from the agencies, and while some were advertising seeds gathered after the temperate summer they'd have sold privately, even before the ads were up. There would only be bulbs now, wherever you went. Daffodils. Crocuses. An occasional luxurious tulip.

'Better than nothing, I suppose.' The old woman raised an eyebrow and sat back again.

Laura's black market bulbs had come from an agency gardener. He'd have been skimming them for weeks to accumulate what he had. Laura bought his entire batch. It cost her everything she had saved from before Connie and then what they gave her after. What they gave all the women who had it done. You got your one chance and then you did as you were told. You couldn't afford not to. It was enough to keep your child fed and at school until twelve years of age. They promised.

Laura was pleased it was daffodils that the black marketeer had. It was exactly what she wanted. There were other yellow flowers but daffodils Laura could plant and leave. She wouldn't have to weed and trim, to pinch out new shoots, or prune. If she couldn't get back in, it didn't matter.

Connie would love it. How she adored yellow. Daffodils. Dandelions. Buttercups. You couldn't pick them even if they were growing right there in the cracks in the pavement and Laura had always scooped Connie into her arms to prevent them getting a fine.

Look at the yellow there.

In the early spring, Laura would walk by this garden and she might hear her say it.

Look at all that yellow. See it? Like lights.

When Laura had planted all but the middle section of the flowerbed the old woman was still there, sitting on the bench. Laura craned her neck. She wanted to see Connie now. She'd never been in a place like this, where she could go off the path. She'd be exploring behind the trees and along the wall. She might have accumulated a pile of conkers, or pushed stones into the dirt, pretending they were seeds.

'You keep looking over at that wall.' The old woman sounded annoyed. 'Perhaps I ought to get you to do some planting there after all. You've got quite a lot in that bed, you know. There's not much room for anything else.'

Laura swallowed. Her saliva tasted sour and angry. 'It's nothing,' she said. 'I was only looking.' She was tired now and the strain of her lie and this thing she had to do made her anxious and irritable. More than anything she wanted the old woman with her private garden and her filtered water to go away. 'As a matter of fact,' Laura heard herself say, 'I thought I saw something.' She pointed at a vine that crawled about the wall. 'Over there.'

The woman sat upright, peering over.

'But I'm sure it's OK,' Laura said, immediately regretting her impulse. 'I mean, I haven't seen anyone come in.'

The woman got up and walked over to where the wall went behind the house. Despite the stick, she walked quickly and steadily. She stood there a while and then returned to the bench. 'You know, there used to be birds nesting in that wall,' she said. She seated herself and sighed. 'I saw the chicks jump out of the nest once, one after the other, but perhaps their wings weren't quite ready. I could hear them calling all day but at night they went quiet and I couldn't hear them any more.'

Laura stopped what she was doing. She wanted to tell Connie. She wanted to show her the place. 'Where was it? Where did they nest?' Laura whispered because she didn't want the woman to stop talking. She was old and perhaps she had forgotten where she was, the things she should not say.

'There was a hole in between the bricks. It must have opened out inside the wall. They landed in amongst the leaves, right there.' She pointed and smiled. 'I never rake out the leaves, old fool that I am.'

For a while neither of them said anything at all. Eventually the old woman must have realised the silence. It was as if she'd been sleepwalking and then woken suddenly, in the middle of a hallway, or leaning out of a window.

'But you can't see the place now,' she said. 'It's all been repointed. And it was such a long time ago. I was only a girl.' She met Laura's eye. 'I wonder sometimes if it was a dream,' she added.

Laura smoothed the soil with her trowel. She didn't want to frighten the woman. You weren't allowed to talk as she had because it had always been like this. It had never been any different.

Laura began to turn the soil in the middle of the bed, digging the holes.

'You mentioned a daughter,' the old woman said. 'Where is she now? Who looks after her when you're gardening?' She sat back in her seat and pushed her stick down hard alongside her leg. Laura checked her stance, her expression. Perhaps she knows, she thought. Perhaps she's guessed. She wishes she hadn't mentioned those birds and now she wants something in return to keep her safe.

Laura was close enough now to take a risk. She was almost finished. She put the trowel down in front of her. 'As a matter of fact, my daughter's here. I brought her with me. I had no choice. You can tell the agency if you like. I'll give you the number when I'm finished.' She looked down at her hands.

There was a pale blank silence. When Laura looked up again the old woman sat in the same position, looking not quite frightened but something rather like it. 'Oh no,' she said. Laura felt her picking her words. 'I was up there watching when you came in. I'd have seen if you had had someone with you.' She dropped her stick. Laura brushed her hands together, leaned over and picked it up for her.

The woman gave her a worried half-smile and Laura felt her palms grow sweaty. She rubbed at one with her thumb and the loose dirt there grew slippery. She put her hand on her bag. 'She was over there, near the wall. Playing near your chestnut tree. I thought she was collecting conkers. But she wouldn't have taken them. She'd never do that.' There were twelve bulbs left. Laura gathered them together and picked up the trowel. 'Don't worry, she'll come now.' She opened the bag and called, 'Connie, Connie,' trying not to sound too desperate. It had to be now. There simply wouldn't be another chance. 'Come over here, Connie. I'm 'nearly done.' Sometimes it worked. Calling out to her, as though nothing was different. Sometimes she appeared.

'Are you sure she was with you when you came in?' The old woman hesitated, then got to her feet. 'I was at my window and I never saw a girl with you.' Her voice fell away as she peered into Laura's bag. It was too late now to hide it. The ceramic pot with its clumsily glazed picture. Laura had chosen one with a tree because there were none with yellow flowers.

'Oh,' the old woman said, stepping back. 'Oh dear.'

Right then, someone appeared at the gate. A man, young, and dressed in an agency uniform. *Perennial Bloom*, his shirt said. He saw them but made a show of searching around the gate for a buzzer.

Laura tried to look at the old woman but it was hard to focus. Her head hurt. She dropped her face into her hands for a moment, inhaling the smell of the soil on her palms. 'Listen,' she said, without looking up, 'I'm just going to put these last twelve in and then I'll leave. I'm not going to do any harm, and this'll take just five minutes to finish.'

The old woman said nothing. Her eyes were moving between the young man at the gate and Laura.

Laura drew her bag in close. It was heavy and dragged at the dirt. She rubbed the fabric of the canvas between her fingers frantically. She could up-end it, and run. What could they do? The gardener would be obliged to complete the planting. The old woman had paid. There would still be a daffodil garden. Briefly, Laura closed her eyes again, but all she could see behind them were flecks of grey, fragments of ash snagging and pulling on concrete and paving stones. She felt her hands reaching out, palms turned down. The words fell away from her.

'Please,' she begged. 'Please let me do this. It's the yellow. I just need to . . . there's nowhere any more. You remember, don't you? I can't find anywhere else.'

She tried to look up at the old woman but found that she couldn't meet her eye. It was a foolish thing she was doing and there were no words to explain it to a stranger.

Laura dropped to her knees and began to gather her tools.

But the old woman was speaking.

'You need to dig a little deeper.' She pointed at Laura's bag. 'Mix it with the soil, then plant those last bulbs in and they'll flower for you.'

She heaved herself up and made her way across the lawn to the gate. From beneath the veil of her hair Laura watched her talking to the young man and when she looked up again he was gone and the old woman was halfway across the lawn. She stopped to caress what must be the peonies before she vanished into the building.

Connie didn't come over but Laura felt certain she was watching. The sun was gone by the time she finished and clouds had gathered. She sat on the bench for a while, looking at the soil, and imagining it aglow with daffodils. When the rain began it was soft and grey and she pulled on a waterproof and listened as the filters on the well started up. Then she packed her bag and left, closing the gate behind her.

VICKY GRUT

Visitors

FIVE TO five on a Friday morning and Hazel lay in bed, waiting to be woken. It was at quiet times like this that the town seemed to press in on her most, hard and unforgiving. Hazel kept her eyes shut and dived back into her dream, where Richard Burton and Elizabeth Taylor were wandering the streets, as they so often did.

Richard Burton wore one of those tweedy jackets with his shirt collar open and a faint shade of stubble on his face. He was drunk – not bloated with beer like the local men, but high-class drunk, with a breath that would burn pure blue if you lit a match. Elizabeth Taylor slouched in a low-cut dress and simple woollen coat, and the two of them wove along together, matching their steps, pulling close and then apart again like gum. You could see they were crazy about each other.

Brando sighed and swam towards Hazel in the bed. Hazel turned away.

In the dream, Richard Burton and Elizabeth Taylor had passed the old bingo hall by now. They turned the corner by the boarded-up shoe shop, went along by the Blind Centre, then past number 10, then number 12. They'd been walking and arguing all night and you could tell they were getting tired. They wanted to stop in somewhere and just sit a while. Let them come here, Hazel willed. Let them choose our house. Let them knock our door. Let them see me – just this once. Brando moved again, reaching up to put an arm around her neck.

'I's awake now, Hazel,' he murmured in his high baby voice.

'Gerroff!' she muttered. But the dream was already lost. She sat up and threw off the covers. 'I was *sleeping*!' His face began to crumple. She leaned in and kissed him quickly. 'Sorry, Brando. Sorry, boy.'

'Brando?' the Vicar had said when her mother had dragged her down to the church to see about a christening. 'Are you sure you're not thinking of Bran? A lovely old Celtic name – or perhaps Brandon as in "from the beacon hill"?'

'No,' said Hazel. 'I'm thinking of Brando as in Marlon Brando.'

'I see,' said the Vicar stiffly. But at least he made no remarks about adultery or fatherless children – not to her face anyway.

By seven o'clock Hazel and Brando were up and dressed. It didn't take long because they hadn't got very undressed the night before. They were fugitives from habit; they were bandits hiding out in this small-town two-up two-down. By seven-ten they were down at the kitchen table eating breakfast while Hazel's mother read the paper.

'Want a bickie,' said Brando.

'No,' said Hazel. 'Eat your toast.'

'Oh, I don't believe it, another disabled person murdered in Cardiff. In their own home, Hazel!'

Hazel made a face of stone.

Brando licked the jam off his toast. It went all over his chin and some strayed up into his hair. 'More, Hazel. Want more stuff on my toast.'

'No,' said Hazel automatically.

'Can't say no, Hazel. Can't say no!'

'You just don't know who you can trust these days, do you?'

Hazel looked away. There was something too big and warm about her mother for the space they had. It hadn't always been like that. She had memories from her childhood of her mother laughing and teasing and full of fun. But somewhere along the line things had got stuck and twisted backwards into this kind of second-hand bloodlust, this passion for other people's suffering. 'Oh my, oh Hazel. Listen to this . . .'

Out in the street Hazel could hear Linda the Milk talking to Melanie next door, clattering the empties.

'. . . little boy wandered away from his mum in a shopping centre. She turned her back for two seconds in the grocer's and next thing he was gone . . . There's pictures of him here on the security cameras . . . "Police fears for his safety are growing." Just a kiddie – not much older than Maggie's boy. Who would do such a thing, eh?'

For some reason Hazel thought about the way she used to wake up at night as a child, afraid that her mother would be dead or gone in the morning. She saw the memory like a piece of film, quite disconnected from herself as she was now: a small child sweating in the dark, holding on to her knees and trying to see the edges of the room, Maggie sleeping softly in the other bed.

'London, this is, Hazel . . .'

Hazel snapped off the picture and made herself think of London instead. She'd been there once when Maggie was a student. The thing she remembered most clearly was the house where Maggie had lived: bare floorboards and two kitchens, one on the ground floor, another on the floor above. That was interesting – odd.

'Think of the poor *mother*, Hazel.'

'Uh.'

'*Think* what she must be *going* through.'

Hazel had a great lurching feeling in her stomach. There was so much pain in the world. It was unbelievable the amount of suffering they lived with all around them. But she couldn't bear the way her mother sat sucking at the horror of it every day, like a maggot feeding on an endless sore. It drove her crazy.

'Want more stuff on, Hazel,' said Brando again.

'No, you've had enough.'

'Can't say no, Hazel,' said Brando earnestly, putting his face up to hers. 'Policeman says, "Can't say no," Hazel.'

She looked at him: hair standing straight up from his face, a streak of green Magic Marker next to one ear, a few strawberry stains from yesterday's tea at the other. She felt a lurch of love.

'I wish you'd get him to call you Mum,' said her mother. 'Children need boundaries.'

After breakfast they went out to the park. Brando couldn't believe his luck. Most days they spent on the sofa watching old films on TV but today Hazel wanted to be away from all the last-minute preparations for Maggie's visit. They went to the pond to watch the ducks and the greedy carp fighting for bread. They looked for ants. They played chase and Batman-and-Robin in the herb garden, and skidded up and down the gravel path by the bandstand. But Hazel's heart wasn't in any of it. And even in the park they weren't safe.

'Morning, Hazel!' called Mrs Thomas, as they passed the bench by the monkey puzzle tree. 'Saw your mother just now, over in Iceland.'

'Yeah?' said Hazel. 'Did she have the huskies with her?'

Mrs Thomas was a bit deaf so she just carried on smiling.

'I expect she's getting a nice bit of chicken for when your sister and her family come, then?'

That knocked all the joke out of Hazel. 'I suppose.'

'I expect she's really been looking forward, then, hasn't she, your mam?' Mrs Thomas showed her crooked teeth again, all gleaming in the sun, greedy for a scrap of someone else's happiness. On another day Hazel would have stopped to talk a bit, because Mrs Thomas was all right really, one of the few who had never been funny about Brando, but today she had no patience for it.

'Yeah well, better be heading back.' Hazel gave a tug at Brando's hand so that he whined. 'Ta-ra then, Mrs T.'

'Mustn't keep you, Hazel,' said Mrs Thomas bravely. 'All the best to your sister, mind.'

What else? said Hazel under her breath: all the best and nothing but.

On the way back Brando grew complaining and overtired. She had to carry him for the last bit and as they turned into their road he fell asleep in her arms. Maggie and Boyd's car was parked outside the house.

Hazel let herself in as quietly as she could. The house was full. She felt as if she had to push against the air to get in through the door. A babble of voices came from the kitchen: Boyd laughing with her dad, the kid shrieking, Maggie and her mam clattering about with plates and cups. Then Boyd and her dad went out in the garden with the kid and the voices in the kitchen dropped to a low murmur.

'Is she still seeing him, do you think?' she heard Maggie ask.

It's amazing how much space a 'family' takes up, thought Hazel. Just one extra person and they use up twice as much space as they should. They probably don't even notice it themselves. They just flatten everything around them.

'Does he have any contact with Brando?'

'To tell you the truth, Maggie, I don't know.' There was a little silence. 'He's back with his wife now, of course.'

Hazel could imagine the look between them.

'And Hazel? Is she still watching all those old films?'

'Day in and day out.'

Silence.

'I've tried, Mags, I really have. I say to her, "What about evening classes?" I say, "Look what an education did for Maggie!" I'd be happy to watch Brando for her, I really would . . .'

'Hi-yah,' Hazel said loudly, stepping out into the middle of the room. Brando was like a sack of lead in her arms but she wouldn't let them see that. She just stood and smiled at them with all her might, her lip snarling up a little at one corner. Her mother looked mortified. Maggie acted as if there was nothing wrong.

'Hazel.' She came up and kissed her sister and laid a hand on the head of the sleeping child. 'You're looking just the same!'

'You look a bit fatter, to be honest,' said Hazel, which was true enough.

Maggie smiled bravely.

'Better put Brando to bed then,' said Hazel.

'Maggie and Boyd and Rupert are in your room again,' her mother called as Hazel climbed the stairs, 'and you two are in with me in the back bedroom. Dad's on the sofa. All right?' (All the best and nothing but.)

On Sunday Brando woke at half past seven. This time Hazel was awake already. She found it hard to sleep in the same bed as her mother. She lay on the edge of the mattress, trying not to roll in and touch that scented flesh. She could barely remember the dream: just the faintest trace of Richard Burton's sulphurous eyes.

She missed Brando. She leaned over the edge and looked at where he lay on a little mattress on the floor.

'Hazel!' he whispered, stretching out his arms. He had a habit of whispering until he was properly awake. It was a nice thing. Hazel slipped down on to the floor and cuddled up next to him. He wriggled his toes with pleasure. He smelled of rancid oil and baby soap. He was so warm. Hazel breathed him in.

'Hazel.'

'Brando.'

She rubbed her nose against his.

'Good boy, Hazel,' Brando murmured sleepily.

In the afternoon she and Maggie went up to the park with the kids. They sat on a bench watching Brando and Rupert play.

'I notice you've got some more pictures up on your wall.'

'Yeah,' said Hazel, reaching for her cigarettes. She didn't trust this careless intimacy. This was Maggie's professional *how're-ya-feeling* voice.

'Richard Burton again, eh?'

'So?'

'You like him, don't you?'

Hazel shrugged. 'Maybe.'

Across the grass in the sandpit, Brando emptied his bucket and handed it to Rupert. Rupert seemed to be explaining something. Brando squatted down beside him, listening with a trusting look. Rupert was a nice enough kid. It wasn't his fault. Perhaps it was just that she wasn't much interested in children apart from Brando.

'They seem to get along, don't they?' Maggie said, following the direction of her gaze.

'I suppose.'

'He's a lovely little lad, Brando.'

'Why wouldn't he be?'

Maggie raised an eyebrow but she didn't seem annoyed. It was the way she was trained, Hazel decided. Maggie was 'handling' her now – just like the crazy people she worked with.

'He looks a lot like you now. Much more than ...' Maggie stopped herself abruptly. '. . . Much more than he did in the first year.'

Hazel drew on her cigarette. She was coiled tight as a spring inside. If Mags says anything more like this, she thought, if she so much as mentions Richard Burton – or John – I'll get up and walk away, real quick, just like I didn't hear.

'I saw him once, you know,' Maggie said in an oddly soft, almost dreamy voice. 'When I was first in London.'

Hazel felt almost sick. She didn't know that John had ever been to London. She tried to raise herself off the bench but somehow her knees wouldn't work.

'It's funny, that – you know, when you see a famous person in real life,' Maggie said in the same disconnected voice.

A famous person? What was she talking about?

'Years ago, this was. When I was still a student. I was walking through Covent Garden, all dressed up in this black silk dress with this beautiful little red-and-gold bolero jacket and my hair cut really short and this hat . . .' Maggie paused for a moment and shook her head. 'The money I wasted on clothes in those days. You wouldn't believe it. Anyway, there I was, feeling really pleased with myself, and I felt this man watching me from the other side of the road. And it was Richard Burton.'

Hazel couldn't think of a single thing to say.

'They were making an advert,' said Maggie. 'They must have been on a break. The crew were fussing about with their equipment and he was standing off to one side in this white linen suit and a panama hat. I had to really look, to make sure, you know, that he was who I thought he was. He wasn't at all embarrassed. He just smiled and gave me a little wave, like this' – Maggie moved her hand against the air in a little wiping motion – 'and then I walked on.'

There was a child on the far side of the park running with a kite. It swooped and failed three or four times, bumping along on its nose, then it caught on a thin ribbon of air and it began to climb, haltingly, behind the running figure.

'It must have been just before he died. I saw the ad on TV later and, if I remember it right, he was already dead when they showed it.'

Even this, thought Hazel, even this she takes away from me. Doesn't she have enough?

'You can always come and stay with us if ever you want to get away, you know that, don't you?'

Hazel jerked her head. 'What do you mean "get away"?' she said tightly.

Across the park, the kite bucked and dipped in the air above the child's head, caught in a cross-current of breezes. The child ran faster, dragging it on.

Maggie tilted her head. 'I can see that this present arrangement has a lot going for it. Mam and Dad really dote on Brando. And I can see that they depend on you a lot in a way, especially now that they're getting older.'

Hazel half turned to her sister in surprise. She'd always thought no one else noticed this.

'It's more you I'm thinking about, Hazel. This is such a small town. In London it wouldn't matter whose kid he was. Nobody would care.'

Neither of them moved for a bit. Hazel thought about London: evil pleasure city; city of houses with two kitchens. At the far side of the park the child came to the end of the fence and stopped in his tracks. The kite began to dip and dive its way to the ground, lodging in the mud like a stricken bird. It didn't seem to occur to him that he could turn around and run back.

'Time to go,' said Hazel briskly, as if she had a rigid schedule to her days. 'Brando needs his tea.'

Maggie got up and followed meekly. Even that was irritating. It costs her nothing to do what I say, thought Hazel.

In the early half-light of Monday morning, Hazel slipped out of her mother's bed and on to the mattress where Brando lay. She closed her eyes and went back to sleep almost at once. This time the dream came easily. She was out in the streets with Richard Burton and Elizabeth Taylor again, listening to the clack of Elizabeth's beautiful shoes on the grey paving stones. Then she was back inside the house, standing in the hallway, listening to their approach. They were sweeping towards her. They were outside the door. They rapped the knocker and she put out her hand to lift the latch and she thought she would burst with the beating of her heart. And she put out her hand . . . And she put out her hand . . .

Hazel sat up suddenly so that Brando tumbled off her in a heap.

'Wakey-wakey, Brando!'

Brando looked surprised.

'Time to get up,' said Hazel fiercely.

They went down to eat breakfast with Maggie, Boyd and Rupert, who were leaving early so that they could miss the traffic on the way back to London. Mam fussed about in the kitchen. Dad went off to the bus station to get the early-morning papers: tabloids for the house, qualities for Maggie and Boyd to take back in the car.

'Sad business in here today,' he said, coming back into the room with a rush of cold air. 'Found his body last night. That little chap in London.'

Mam's eyes were black caverns of despair. She stood looking out at her family. 'Oh no!'

Hazel jerked her head away.

'Poor little mite.' Mam leaned over the picture of the smiling face on the front page, one hand clutching the dressing gown to her breast. 'Such wickedness. Poor lamb. No older than our Rupert. What chance . . .? Innocent defenceless little . . .'

Brando crawled up on to Hazel's lap and she buried her face in his hair. She had to open her mouth to get her breath. She didn't want to be like her mother. But somehow the tears came anyway, flooding up from some well-hidden dam inside her.

Maggie got up and put her arms around her mother.

'You will be careful, won't you, love? You will take care of Rupert, won't you? You will make sure he's never alone or . . .'

129

'Don't worry, Mam. We're fine,' and Maggie rocked her mother against her like a child.

Boyd and Dad packed the car and Mam took Rupert with her for a last check in the upstairs rooms for forgotten toys and stray socks.

'You'll think about what we talked about yesterday, won't you?' said Maggie. 'About visiting?'

Hazel hesitated.

'Don't be put off by that news story,' Maggie said quickly. 'London's no more dangerous than anywhere else. It could have happened anywhere.'

Hazel thought of Maggie being in London when she was young, and Richard Burton watching her. She remembered why she had followed Maggie around everywhere once and wanted to be like her. Perhaps I will do it, thought Hazel. She felt a sudden spurt of energy, as if a door opened a little bit inside her head again. She thought how light and easy she would feel in a place where nobody knew her: away from John and his wife and the watching streets.

'Maybe,' she said, grinning.

'Do it!' whispered Maggie, squeezing her hand. 'Come soon.'

As the car disappeared around the corner, Hazel let her mother put an arm about her. 'They'll be back in a couple of months,' she said lamely. Hazel allowed herself to be hugged.

Mam shook her head. 'You never stop worrying about your children, whatever age they are. You'll understand how I feel one day, Hazel. You're a mother yourself now.'

'Yes,' said Hazel. They stood for a moment looking out at the road, then her mother turned slowly back to the house. One day I will be like that, thought Hazel, and Brando will be like Maggie: driving away to somewhere else.

Brando dropped down on his haunches on the front step, his hands clutched across his stomach.

'Ants,' he said seriously.

'Uh huh,' said Hazel.

She could feel the very small flash of will to escape flickering out. Maggie would think that it was because of John but it wasn't. She didn't even think about John that much any more. It was more that she felt she wouldn't belong anywhere else but here. She'd overheard the Vicar saying once, 'If they don't leave the Valleys by the time they're eighteen, they never get away.' Perhaps there was something in that.

Richard Burton was leaning against the Santoris' house across the street, smoking. 'Ah, come on now, Hazel,' he said in his half-wheedling, half-fighting tone. 'It's not such a bad old town, is it now?' Hazel ignored him. She didn't need Richard Burton butting in on things right now.

The parking-meter man was working his way down the street (it had gone residents-only-parking now). At the other end of the street, Mrs Collins and Mrs Edwards slowed to get a good look at what was going on. Brando was lying on his stomach on the pavement saying, 'Where's *my* ant, Hazel? Where's it gone?'

Mrs Collins and Mrs Edwards said something to each other now and shook their heads. Hazel stepped out and gave them her fighting look, which got rid of them quick enough.

'So you made a mistake,' said Richard Burton, not following her train of thought.

'No I did not!' Hazel snapped.

'So we all make mistakes. Sometimes the mistakes are the best part. So we go back and make them again. And again.' Richard Burton tossed his fag-end into the gutter and glanced up at the upstairs front bedroom where old Mrs Santori used to sleep before they took her off to the home. Elizabeth Taylor was standing by the window in her wedding dress, looking beautiful and pretending not to know it. Richard Burton winked at Hazel. 'That's life, isn't it, though, Hazel? You can travel far and wide and see nothing, and you can stay at home and see it all. Isn't that so?'

In the upstairs room, behind the net curtains, Elizabeth Taylor spun around a few times, just for fun.

'Maybe so,' said Hazel, 'more than you want.'

'*There's* it!' Brando cried triumphantly. 'I got my ant, Hazel. Look!'

From deep inside the house Hazel could hear her mother calling them. She knew there'd be a fresh pot of tea on the table by now, her father dozing in the easy chair and Mam rustling at the pages of the day's news. She could always go in and put the TV on for a bit. They might be showing a 1930s comedy or a 1940s B-movie. It would pass the time. Hazel glanced back at the house, then out to the road.

'Look, Hazel,' Brando said again. And Hazel looked. Brando stood with his arm outstretched, showing her the ant in the cup of his hand, his head tipped back so that the fringe fell away from his head in waves, his feet planted squarely on the pavement – all flesh and blood and colour and not going anywhere yet. And suddenly she didn't give a toss about Richard Burton or Elizabeth Taylor, or any other dead thing that didn't really belong to her.

She grabbed his hand. 'Forget the ant, Brando. Get your coat.'

'Why, Hazel?'

'Because we're going out, boy. Just you and me. We're going out and we're going to have ourselves the best of days.'

ALISON DUNN

Omi's Ghosts

B AD MEN talk about the ghosts they've made but they don't go to sleep in the dark. Omi made three ghosts by the time he was fifteen and I knew he went to bed with the lamp turned down low, enough to keep them at bay. I can see him lying on his bed in his tiny bedroom with the wardrobe door half falling off and shirts hanging out, Marley poster taped to the wall and his school books dumped on the floor. His purple Yankees cap dipped down over his eyes hitting the bridge of his nose. His long arms and long fingers reaching out to change the lamplight when he felt uncomfortable, when he felt those ghosts coming. I'm lying in my bed starting to wonder if Omi wasn't right in thinking like he did and I'm wishing I had my own lamp. I'm sixteen next Wednesday and I'm no bad man. When I'm older I want a fowl farm and a popcorn machine, but right now I don't want to sleep in the dark either.

When I first held a gun I was eight. I was in a car park in Trench Town with Omi kicking round a football in the dirt after it rained and a bad man gave me it and said, 'You know wah dis is?'

I said, 'Yes,' and he said, 'Point it to dat man.'

So I pointed it. The gun was cold and heavy and my arm hurt to hold it up.

The man said, 'You, little boy, you is a bad boy.'

Omi started laughing and turning around and around in circles like a mad dog. The man took it back and walked away towards his blue Ford. I ran two blocks to our house and I sat on my bed until Ma came in from work. The iron roof expanded and cracked under the sun making me jump even though I knew what it was. I didn't want to be like a bad man, but I felt like one. I sniffed my fingers to see if there was gunpowder on them, but they only smelled of corn chips.

Omi and I, we knew each other since we were babies, born six months apart. Our homes were eight little dirty pieces of land away from each other on West Road and our mas used to meet up in the daytime until we had to go to school. Omi's ma used to bring Omi's baby sister and sit and sew clothes in the shade, talking chit-chat with my ma. We played in the dirt round the back of the house and the washroom. They were these low buildings with crumbling walls and iron roofs and black water ran on the ground by our knees from twenty backyards up the street. We'd make things with the broken bits of concrete, old pieces of metal and busted tyres lying around. The best thing we ever built was a replica of the street we lived on with all the little details like the church and the drugstore and the women who sell sweets on the side of the road. The potholes they made themselves.

Omi told me he was seven the first time he held a gun. His ma sent him to the cistern to catch water one afternoon. A man who lived a few houses down jumped the fence. He told Omi to give way so he could wash his hands and he gave him the gun. The dogs were barking at him and the bad man said, 'Dem dogs are like informers. I just killed a man and dey come in like dey want to kill me.'

But the police didn't come that time. Omi was smiling

as he was telling me and he said the gun felt nice when he held it.

By the time I was ten, I was hiding under the bed every night when I heard the gunshots, trying to block out the noise. But I was bragging to every boy who'd listen, 'Me nah 'fraid. Big man give me gun to hold, middle-size man give me gun to hold, little youth give me gun to hold. Every man wan' me to hold their gun.'

It always happened when I was with Omi. It must have been something about him that pulled them like a magnet. One time after school we were on the street by the bread shop and a man with a gold front tooth gave us a gun to hold. He was a bad man, he had just killed someone and the police were after him. He told us to run and hide the gun.

'I need to go wash mih hands,' he said.

Everyone needs to go wash their hands. We ran across the street, down the alley and hid it under a big stone by the ackee tree. If the police had seen us with the gun, they would have killed us. Those times we didn't know that much about guns.

Omi and I were playing football after school one Monday and he said, 'Marvin, you wanna fire a gun? Not to shoot someone off, but just bus one out of it?'

I didn't want to be soft, so I said, 'Yeah, man.'

'Come with me and see Carlton.'

'Who's Carlton?'

'He's my general.'

'You got a general? Since when?'

'Since last night.'

Omi looked so proud, he swung his leg and bounced his step all the way to the corner of Burke Road and Spanish Town Road. There was about ten of them sitting on the pavement drinking tea. My legs shook and I knew I was soft.

'I gotta go, Omi. See you tomorrow,' and I ran all the way home and sat on the bed again. I didn't look back at him once.

Omi didn't get home that night until late and I don't know how she knew or if she knew but Omi's ma beat him so hard her hands swelled up as if there was water around them. She beat him with anything she could find: a belt, a board and her flat fat palms. He came to school with a blue face, puffed-up lips and a cut above his eyebrow. Omi's father was a rum-head drinker and left when he was two. His mother had to grow all six of them on her own. She must have had something boiling up in her to do that to Omi.

I didn't see him so much after that. Every day after school, every weekend, every holiday, Omi was sitting with those boys on the corner, eating, drinking, playing cricket, playing football. That gang, they looked after Omi and gave him lunch money, told him to wear his uniform like his own father would but better. I didn't need no lunch money, my mother gave me it every day. My father was mostly in Spanish Town, but he sent money back every now and then. I didn't need them like Omi needed them.

Bad things happened to Omi when he ran with them, though. They weren't just some corner crew with guns looking after a lane and acting like they were men because their daddies weren't around. They were bad men with drugs, cocaine from Colombia coming through Kingston to London. They shot you dead then apologised afterwards. Worst thing I heard was that one of them killed a little girl on the way to school in her blue uniform. She was the baby sister of some bad man challenging their turf. Omi spent too much time down there. Before long he was obligated to them so that he did anything they wanted. I still saw him at school, he was still my best friend, but I know he didn't tell me everything that happened to him.

Omi got a girl. Soon enough this bad man called Bulldog – he used to be part of Carlton's gang until he broke away on his own turf to do his own business – he had sex with Omi's girl and sent her back crying and all messed up. Omi couldn't tell the police because Bulldog would come and kill him straight up for being an informer. So Omi decided to shoot him himself. I didn't hear that from Omi, I heard that from Patrick at the drugstore. Omi went and shot Bulldog in the head four times in his own home. He told me he made his first ghost and I just didn't know what to say to him. He stood there all tall over me and his eyes didn't look quite like Omi's any more.

The next week, mid-afternoon on a Saturday in their home, Omi's sister got eight shots on her body and she died there in his hands. He watched her crying and his ma crying and he couldn't do nothing. My ma heard the shots when she was hanging up the washing on the line outside, she heard the crying and the ambulance come with its sirens wailing. She told me she put her hands over her ears it was so terrible to listen. I went around the next day and said I was sorry for his loss.

Omi said to me, 'If you see someone tek someone's life, it's like a space has gone and you have to tek revenge.'

The violence, it makes you bad, it makes you want revenge. You grow up and you don't want to be a bad man, but you can't let them kill yours without you killing theirs. There are too many guns here; they come through from America and our dirty politicians give them to our foot soldiers in the garrisons to make sure they get them votes. The next thing we got guns on every street corner, kids like me and Omi holding guns at seven years old. Guns, cocaine, arriving and flying, but some sticking, like Kingston is about the easiest through road in a global village bent on getting high. The police, they talk about peace but they don't do it the right way. All they do is bring in more police cars and bigger weapons; they don't give us anything to do.

Omi found out the bad man who killed his sister and he poured gas on this man's house so it burned down with his mother and grandmother inside. It seems too much, the violence, but it don't stop. Omi started boasting about the ghosts he'd made and I guessed it wouldn't be long.

Three days later, a Tuesday, just after lunch, it was quiet on the street. I was in the drugstore with Patrick drinking tea and we were talking about the Arnett Gardens and Rivoli United match. Omi walked right past the door, straight-bodied, with his chin up and his cap pulled down low over his forehead. I pushed my head through the doorway and called out, 'Hey, Omi!'

He turned around without slowing his pace and waved at me with his long arm high in the air and carried on. It wasn't like him; he usually stopped for me, no matter what he was doing. I closed the drugstore door and looked through the window with Patrick. A black BMW turned slowly into the street from behind Omi's back. Omi must have sensed something. He looked left and right sharply and couldn't find anywhere to turn. He quickened his step with his head down and the car picked up speed. It rolled past the drugstore. There were two men in the front seats. I turned my head away so they wouldn't see me looking at them. When I turned back Omi had started running. The driver revved the engine and accelerated hard down the tarmac.

Omi tried to find somewhere to go. He bounced left and right again like his feet were tricking him not knowing which way to run. He punched on the door of the old bakery but it was boarded up a long time ago. The car drove level with him. The man in the passenger seat jabbed the gun out of the window. Omi crossed his arms over his face and turned his back. There were three shots – blam, blam, blam. Omi turned round in a circle, his legs twisting and his arms flying up in the air. The driver accelerated hard and the back wheels of the car spun up a dust cloud.

It was quiet for a second. The second after Omi was shot was the quietest I ever heard that road. Then I heard myself shouting like I was underwater, 'Omi. Omi. Omi.'

My arms shook, my legs shook, I scrabbled down the road with so much trouble I thought the earth was moving under my feet. Omi was lying twisted up, his tripe pouring out. I tried to put my arms around his neck but his body was limp and my shirt soaked up his blood. Patrick pulled me away by my shoulders.

'Marvin, it's too late.'

Omi's cap was lying on the ground and I picked it up. We both knelt there in his blood, looking at him. His face was like he was sleeping; he had a bit of dirt stuck to his cheek and I wiped it off. I had tears spilling down my face like water from a broken rain pipe. Some women were standing over us for a while peering and weeping. One of them whispered a prayer all softly and ended it 'God rest his soul' and when she said 'Amen' they all joined in. Their shadows darkened Omi's face and I waved them away.

The dead truck never wanted to pick him up. The driver called the next one and the next one took him to the morgue. I had to go and tell Omi's ma that I saw it all happen and that I couldn't do nothing. She tried to be brave but as I left their backyard I heard her wail a hole in the sky. I couldn't eat for three days even though I saw it coming like Tuesday follows Monday.

I lie on my bed at night and I think of Omi lying in his bed with his cap pulled down over the bridge of his nose. I know that someone made Omi's ghost and now it's me that don't sleep in the dark. I don't want to be a bad man but, like Omi said, I saw someone take someone's life and now there's a space. I just don't know what Omi would want me to do.

Thank you to the work of Joy Moncrieffe: 'The making and unmaking of the shotta (shooter): boundaries and (counter) actions in the "garrisons" ', IDS Working Paper 297, Institute of Development Studies, Brighton.

YIYUN LI

Number 3, Garden Road

THEY HAD moved into number 3, Garden Road forty-five years ago, he with his new wife, she with her parents and three younger siblings. Garden Road was a narrow dirt lane then, a patch of radish field on one side, wheat on the other. Number 3, a four-storey, red-brick building, was the first to be built. The first to be numbered also, though no reason had ever been given about not starting from the very beginning. To this day Garden Road, a four-lane thoroughfare with its many shops and flat buildings on both sides, missed the first two numbers, a fact known to few people, and number 3, its red façade darkened by dust and soot and cracked by a major earthquake twenty years ago, stood irrelevantly between two high-rise buildings with consecutive numbers, an old relative that no one could identify in a family picture.

Of all the residents in the building, Mr Chang and Meilan were the only ones remembering the hot July day forty-five years ago, when government-issued furniture – tables, chairs, desks, beds, painted brownish yellow with numbers written underneath in red – had been unloaded from flatbeds and assigned to the new tenants. Mr Chang was in his mid-twenties then, a young recruit for the newly established research institute to build the first missile for the country. As he was waiting for his share of furniture, a toddler from a neighbour's family wobbled over and placed a sticky palm on his knee. Uncle Fatty, she called him, looking up with a smile innocent and mysterious at once. He was a stout young man but far from being fat; still, when the crowd laughed out of their approval for the child's wit, he knew that the nickname would stay.

Apart from Mr Chang's new wife, Meilan was perhaps the only other one who had noticed his embarrassment. Meilan was ten then, and it was the first time she saw a man blushing. It was her youngest sister who had given Mr Chang the nickname, so there was no other choice for Meilan but to use the name, too. Calling someone not much older than her Uncle was enough of a torture; the name, Uncle Fatty, troubled her long after it had stopped bothering him.

Uncle Fatty and his wife lived in a unit directly above Meilan's family. A natural musician, he played different string instruments: violin, er-hu, pi-pa, and an exotic one Meilan had never seen. Music from that instrument, unlike the graceful serenades from the violin or the weeping folk songs from the er-hu and the pi-pa, was loud with happy beats, but it was those songs that had broken Meilan's heart to pieces before she had known it.

Forty-five years was a long time, enough to broaden the muddy, nameless creek next to Garden Road into a man-made river, named Moon River after an American love song and adding value to the already rocket-high price of properties on Garden Road. 'Ten thousand yuan per square metre now. Last year it was only eight thousand,' Meilan said whenever there was a newcomer to the dancing party at the riverside park. Units at number 3 had been up for sale twelve years ago when private-owned housing had been made legal. Meilan's parents had asked their children for help so that they would not lose their home, and Meilan had been the only one to withdraw all her savings to assist the purchase. Naturally her siblings had thought it her duty then, as she had just moved back with her parents after her second divorce. It had turned out to be a wise investment, and for that her siblings had written her off as an opportunist.

'Thirty thousand yuan in '95. With that amount of money I could buy half of a bathroom in this neighbourhood nowadays,' Meilan said often, shaking her head in happy disbelief. Like many of the street dancing parties in Beijing, the gathering by Moon River – the Twilight Club it was called – was attended mostly by old people, and repetitions were tolerated as they would not be elsewhere with children and grandchildren. A lucky bird she was, one of those men who liked to nod at everything Meilan said would compliment her when she mentioned her real estate success. Lucky she was, she would reply, with no children to break her back, no husband to break her heart.

Meilan was the youngest and slimmest woman at the Twilight Club, indulged by men ten or twenty years her senior. Little Goldfish, they called her, even though she was past the age for such a girlish nickname. Indeed when she plunged into the music she felt like a playful fish, one of her regular partners holding her tight while his wife, no longer able to match his energy and enthusiasm, watched on among a group of women her age, not without alarm. Once in a while a wife would comment that Meilan did not belong to the Twilight Club. 'Go to a nightclub, or a karaoke bar,' the wife would urge. 'Show the young people what is called ageing gracefully.'

Meilan smiled good-naturedly, but the next time she

danced with a man whose wife had tried to offend her she embraced him tightly and whispered so that he had to put his ear, already hard of hearing, close to her lips.

The only man Meilan had not danced with at the Twilight Club was Mr Chang, though between the two of them they had missed no more than a handful of parties in the past twelve years. In fact, it was Mr Chang who had introduced Meilan to the Twilight Club. She had recently returned to live with her parents then, middle-aged and twice-divorced, without a child from either husband to soften people's criticism. To kill the time after work and to escape her parents' nagging, Meilan took to strolling along Moon River, and on one of those first evenings since her return she discovered Mr Chang, sitting on a bench with a woman. He did not recognise Meilan when her gaze caught his eyes, and the woman, in her red blouse and golden skirt, was not the beautiful wife who had, many years ago, made Meilan conscious of her own less attractive features.

Uncle Fatty, Meilan's parents reported when she queried about him, had stayed in number 3. His wife had been ill with some sort of cancer for the last year or so. Is she still alive? Meilan asked with great interest, and her parents, shocked by her inappropriate curiosity, replied that they were too old to discuss other people's health problems with the unfeeling young generation.

Now that she knew he had a wife somewhere – dying in a hospital, or at the mercy of a brusque caretaker in their unit – Meilan started to follow Mr Chang in the evenings. He left home at half past six and went to the nearest bus stop to meet his lady friend. They strolled along Moon River, now and then resting on an available bench and talking in low voices. Twice a week they went to the Twilight Club and danced all night till the last song,

'Long Live Friendship', its archaic Chinese lyrics set to the tune of 'Auld Lang Syne'. The first time Meilan watched a hundred old people slow-dance to the song, she was overwhelmed by bleakness that she had never known exist nor had been prepared to understand. In her adulthood Meilan was considered by many as a woman without much depth; brainless she had been called behind her back by her siblings, the kind of wife made for a cheating husband.

Meilan was caught off guard by her tears, and she had to hide behind a bush when the partygoers bid farewell to one another. Later, when she followed Mr Chang and his lady friend to the bus stop, Meilan was pleased that 'Auld Lang Syne' had not moved him to hail a cab for the woman with whom he was perhaps thinking of replacing his wife.

The woman soon was replaced by a younger, prettier-looking woman, who did not last long. A couple more women later, his wife died, but the news was a few weeks old when it reached Meilan. She did not remember having detected any sadness in Mr Chang; at least there had not been any change in his evening routine. By then she had created a few opportunities to encounter him in the building, but he only nodded at her in the same unrecognising manner as if she had been one of those less fortunate who had to rent in number 3. She studied herself in the mirror. Even if his deteriorating eyesight and memory prevented him from recognising her from her girlhood, she did not see why she could not compete with the women he was dancing with twice a week. Perhaps she only needed a different setting to meet him instead of their dusty, stale-smelling hallway. Meilan spent half a month of pay to take a dancing class, and after that she showed up at the Twilight Club like a princess. The hem of her long skirt brushed the sandalled feet of her partners in the summer, and in winter they competed to hold her hands nestled in a pair of white suede gloves. Little Goldfish, soon the men renamed her; there was no excuse for Mr Chang not to see her and perhaps desire her in ways she did not care to imagine.

The Twilight Club had become a centre of Meilan's life. She accepted small harmless presents and dinner invitations from men with wives, but once a widower made a move to differentiate himself from her other admirers, she discouraged him with subtle yet resolute gestures. In time death came for some of the old men, but one only had to avert one's eyes to forget such inconvenient disruptions. With a flat, a small pension, and many admirers, Meilan had little more to ask from life. If there was one imperfection, it would be Mr Chang – what right did he have to ignore her for twelve years, all while he was busy dancing with those not so young women who had to take buses to the Twilight Club?

Mr Chang circled the flat: the kitchen, the living room, the bedroom their twin boys used to share. He slept in one of the single beds now. The other bedroom, where he had spent thirty-three years of his married life with his wife, was entered every spring and autumn when he took her clothes out on to the balcony for airing. Once upon a time the lingering scent of sunshine on the clothes, mixed with that of the camphor, had filled the flat with a peculiar presence of another warm body and left Mr Chang drowsy for days afterwards; now that number 3 was dwarfed on both sides by high-rises and Garden Road was congested often with a long queue of honking cars, the clothes came home with a cold strangeness to the touch. The liveliness that took longer to leave the clothes than for a body to be cremated, a slower death, made Mr Chang wonder how much he had not known about life, which he had once thought of coming to completion at the deathbed of his wife.

Mr Chang poured tea for himself. Each time he finished a circuit of the flat he swallowed another pill with half a cup of tea. At least an hour of his morning would be covered by the handful of pills. Another two hours by the three morning newspapers to which he subscribed. Cooking, an hour, and eating, with the new, ill-fitted denture, another half-hour. The afternoons were less intimidating, for he allowed himself to nap as long as he could. The evening papers arrived a little before four o'clock, and by half past six, with some leftover from lunch in his stomach and clean clothes on, he was ready to meet his friend at the bus stop.

They were always his friends – not girlfriends as many of them might have mistakenly thought – coming into his life and then leaving, one at a time. Some of them were easier to break up with than others; one of them, about five years ago, had gone to the extreme of threatening to kill herself for him, but he had known, as she had too, the flimsiness of the threat. Passion of that sort could only be taken seriously when one was in one's twenties, a novice of love and of life in general. And not to his surprise, even the most persistent ones among the women eventually left him alone. After all, there had not been any intimate touches to be accounted for; he had only strolled along Moon River and danced at the Twilight Club with them. It was they who had nurtured their own hope, even if they could blame him for misleading them in the first place.

When an old friendship came to an end, a new one began without a problem. For the records Mr Chang kept at a dozen matchmaking agencies, the few key details he provided – a retired scientist, with a sizeable pension and a flat on Garden Road – were enough to attract certain women. He did not go through the big binders to choose someone but let his name remain to be chosen by desperate women, with whom he had not many specific requirements except for two rules: he was not to go out with a mother – a child could be a complication in time, and he had brought up two sons of his own and had no intention to help with raising another child, grandchildren included; and he would not befriend a woman who had never married. Divorced women in their middle age, with no housing of their own nor great jobs for long-term stability, was all he needed – enough of them were plagued by their futures in this city and there was no reason to put his peace at stake by wading to the more treacherous water.

Mr Chang had never thought of remarrying, though for a while his fellow dancers at the Twilight Club thought one or other of his friends would become his new wife. They complimented him on his ability to attract women who were fifteen or twenty years younger than him, and perhaps secretly they also envied him for the many opportunities they themselves did not have. In time some of them joined him in his widowhood, and a few of them remarried, joking with him of their taking the lead now. Mr Chang smiled, but eventually, as he had expected, people started to treat him more as a joke. An old donkey who loved to chew on the fresh grass, they must have been saying behind him. He'd better watch out for his stomach, some of them would perhaps say, but they forgot it was the heart that would kill a man; a man never died from indigestion.

In late April the regulars at the Twilight Club decided to change the party schedule and meet four times a week instead of twice. Spring in Beijing was as brief as a young girl's grief over a bad haircut and they might as well have a good grip of the season before the sauna weather set in, though no doubt by then they would have more reasons to keep the schedule despite the heat. Amid the excitement the absence of Mr Chang went unnoticed except by Meilan, and when he didn't show up for the next two parties she decided that it was her responsibility as a neighbour to check on him.

A little before five she knocked on his door. It was a decent time for a single woman to drop in at a widower's, with dinner as an available excuse if the meeting was unpleasant. She had put on her favourite silk blouse of sapphire blue and a matching skirt, secretly hoping that, if she were not to find Mr Chang in grave illness, they would perhaps show up at the Twilight Club together that night.

Mr Chang looked alarmed when he opened the door, his round-neck undershirt and threadbare pants reminding her of her own father in his old age. 'Little Goldfish?' he said. Though the question was inappropriate for a greeting she was glad that he recognised her.

She told him her name, and he showed little recollection. 'I'm the first daughter of Lu's downstairs,' Meilan said. 'Remember, Uncle Fatty? My little sister gave you the name.'

He had to excuse himself to change into more formal clothes so that he could calm himself. His wife had always called him by that name; Aunt Fatty, he would reply with forced cheerfulness, till the very end of her life when her body had been wasted by the cancer. One would hope for certain things to be buried, but no, a woman whom he did not want to dance with would come and knock on his door, claiming her partial ownership of a name she had no right to use. Mr Chang's hands shook when he buttoned his shirt. If he lay down on the single bed would the woman take the cue from the closed bedroom door and leave him alone? But she would break into the bedroom, she would call an ambulance if he insisted on ignoring her questions, and no doubt she would, later at the Twilight Club, brag about how she saved his life by being a considerate neighbour.

Windows in his unit opened to the same view as hers did, and Meilan was surprised that she had overlooked this fact despite the time she had spent imagining his life. The last time she had visited the unit she had been twelve, and in the living room there had been a few articles of furniture identical to theirs. She wondered if he had sold the ugly-coloured furniture with red-painted numbers underneath. Her own parents had saved every piece, but after their deaths she had hired two labourers to dispose of the furniture as they willed. She regretted now that she hadn't saved a few pieces; had there ever been an opportunity for him to pay her back a visit, the furniture might have provided shared memories, a topic of conversation.

Mr Chang entered the living room, and Meilan did not turn from where she stood in front of the window. 'Remember the pigsties?' she said, lifting her chin at a man washing his brand-new Lexus in the narrow lane between number 3 and the next building. The pigsties had been there in 1977 when she had come home to her parents with the news of her first divorce. The man worked on diligently, unaware that he was being watched as full pens of pigs had once been watched from the windows of number 3.

Mr Chang sat down on the couch before the guest did. An ill-mannered host, she must be thinking of him, but he had not invited her, and he would let her draw her own conclusions. Of the women at the Twilight Club he had avoided her more than others. A rabbit should not chew on the grass around his nest, Mr Chang had told a few old men when they had hinted that, as neighbours, he and Little Goldfish could develop a convenient romance. They had laughed at his cunning reply, but they, unwise old souls who could be deceived by a flirtatious gesture from a no-longer-young woman, could not see that certain women, Little Goldfish being one of them, were to be shunned for their shrewdness.

'We used to name the pigs after people in number 3,' Meilan said and turned around with a smile. 'Of course you were one of the grown-ups then, so you wouldn't know our tricks.'

'I didn't know you moved back,' Mr Chang said.

'I bought the unit downstairs for my parents,' she said. 'They didn't want to live elsewhere.'

The same with his wife and him, Mr Chang replied, though it was only half the truth. They had helped both sons with their purchases of their bigger, more modern flats so they could marry their dream lovers, and in the end number 3, with its rumbling pipes and cracking walls and garbage chute that still attracted flies years after it had been sealed, was what Mr Chang and his wife could afford.

Meilan nodded and sauntered to the couch. He stood up quickly and watched her take the seat close to where he had been sitting. Tea, he asked, and when she said yes, he was both horrified at her insistence in extending the visit and relieved that he had an excuse to leave the room. When he returned from the kitchen he sat down in an armchair across the room.

He had his shirt on now, buttoned to the top, and Meilan had to restrain herself from reminding him that his shirt tail was escaping from his belt. The glass top of the coffee table had tea stains; a bowl of leftover noodle soup was sitting on a pile of newspapers. The flat was not one where a man could entertain a lady friend; she felt an urge to absolve him of all the women he had danced with.

'I heard about your wife's passing,' Meilan said, eyeing the framed pictures of his wife on the wall, mostly enlarged black-and-white snapshots, taken, judging from the clothes and the young look of the wife, before anyone in number 3 had been able to afford colour films. It was strange to study his wife through an older woman's eyes; years ago her beauty had been stifling to Meilan, but now she detected melancholy in the young face. Such a woman would let herself be defeated by an illness. 'A good wife you had,' Meilan said. 'I'm sorry about your loss.'

It had been eleven years but the way she said it made the pain fresh again. He had been sad to hear about her parents' passing, too, he said, as if by reminding her of her own loss he would be spared. It was different with one's parents, she argued, and he had little to defend himself. The tea kettle whistled, a prompt excuse for him to withdraw from her gaze.

'Have you thought of remarrying?' Meilan asked when he returned with the tea.

She must have seen his friends at the Twilight Club so it was natural for her to regard him as an old donkey fond of fresh grass. It was better that she, or anyone in the world, think that way. He shook his head without giving more explanation. Instead, he asked her about her marriage and her children as if it were a game of ping-pong that one had to win with tactful performance.

'No husband, no child.'

'You own a flat on Garden Road,' he said weakly. There was little else to compliment her on.

'Funny thing is, we moved here when I was ten, so there must have been another home before this one but I don't remember it,' Meilan said. 'Am I not a lucky one to die in the only home I've known?' It was meant to be a joke, but she was surprised to see that he looked pale and shaken. She had always liked to talk about her own death as if it was an event to look forward to, her secret superstition being that death, like a man, would make himself conveniently unavailable once he knew he was desired.

The only home for him, too, he thought. His sons had tried to persuade him to sell the unit in number 3 after his wife's death and he had refused. It was not his responsibility to make them understand him; time would come and teach them about love that they thought they had known already.

Meilan studied the old man shrinking into the depth of the armchair, his eyes looking past her and dwelling on some distant past she had no place in. How many times in his life had he let himself truly see her? She remembered years ago – when gas pipes had not been installed in number 3 and when propane tanks had been rationed – she had often hidden behind a pile of coal bricks on the third-floor landing and waited for Uncle Fatty to come back from work. How old was she then? Twelve, or perhaps thirteen, too old to play in the sooty hallway, but she persisted. Once a rat came out from nowhere and jumped on to the coal, not more than five feet from where she squatted. Neither the rat nor Meilan moved for a long moment until Uncle Fatty and his wife walked upstairs. The rat scurried away, frightening his wife in its swift movement, and Meilan remembered him looking past her to search for the offender. She had been born ten years too late to bear any meaning to him, she remembered weeping to her journal.

'I've always thought that one of your lady friends will be good enough to marry into number 3,' Meilan said, laughing lightly. 'Have you realised you're the only one to bring your own partner to the Twilight Club?'

He would no longer bring a woman, but such information he did not have to share with a stranger. His wife had told him to start searching for a replacement since the relapse of her cancer; she would like to see him taken care of so she could leave in peace, she had said. He obliged her as one would oblige any fantasy of a dying loved one, but he could not stop himself from strolling and dancing with strangers after her death. He would do anything to keep her alive from day to day, even if it meant being called an old donkey and using other women's hope as an anaesthesia. A week ago, when he had had to break up with his latest friend and call the matching agencies, none of the agencies had provided any new names who had shown interest in his file. A clerk at one of the agencies had even suggested that he no longer pay the fee to keep his file active; her words were subtle but there was no way to make the message less humiliating.

'Of course everything gets harder at our age,' Meilan said. Ten years could be an abyss when one was twelve years old, and what a relief one did not have to stay twelve all one's life. She adjusted her necklace of cultured pearls and sipped the tea. 'So if you ask me, I'd say you're the smartest. It's better just to have a few dances together. Beyond that things get complicated and unworthy.'

'So you've always been single?' Mr Chang asked with some curiosity. The woman, uninvited and at ease in his home, was different from his friends. Was it because she owned the patch of roof above her?

'Married twice, lost twice to mistresses,' she said. 'No, you don't have to feel sorry for me. The way I look at it – a bad marriage is like a bad tooth and it's better to remove it than suffer from it.'

Mr Chang leaned forward. He had some vague recollection of her from years ago, but hard as he tried, he could not connect the woman to the young girl, whom his wife had once commented on as being intense and sad for her age. He had never doubted his wife, for whom the world seemed to be more transparent, many of its secrets laid out for her to see, but could she have made a mistake about the girl, or had time alone been able to transform a sad and serious girl into a loud and graceless woman?

'To think about it, at least I don't have to grieve over the death of a spouse,' Meilan said. She was insensitive, she knew, but why would she want to pretend to be someone other than herself, even for him?

'That's to be congratulated,' he said with sincerity, but perhaps she took it as a sarcastic comment, as she shrugged without replying.

The light dimmed in the flat. Evenings in Mr Chang's unit, as in Meilan's, came early in all seasons, their windows shadowed by the high-rise next door. In the soft light Meilan fixed her eyes on his face, unscrupulously. 'What would your wife have said about your lady friends?'

She had told him that he needed another woman in his life so she could rest in peace; would she have less peace had she known that not one but many had been in his life, coming and going? Mr Chang shook his head. 'The dead are gone, the living live on,' he said. The same saying must have been quoted by all the widows and widowers in this city when they accepted a substitution.

'The living live on only to ignore a long-time neighbour,' Meilan said. She wondered if she had sounded like a hurt woman. What she meant, she said, was that they were both good dancers, and wasn't it a surprise that they had never danced together? Unless there was more than a dancing partner he had been searching for, she added with laughter; she herself had no interest in anything other than dancing, she explained, dancing being all that mattered to her.

The woman, with her cunning smile as if she had seen through him, looked familiar. Mr Chang felt a moment of disgust mixed with fascination. Then it came to him, not the woman in front of him but another one, with her hand between his legs, not moving much but nevertheless one could detect the pressure from each of her fingers. He had been thirteen then, taking a train ride for the first time in his life to the provincial capital for middle school; the other passengers, his uncle included, had been dozing off in the dimming light of the northern plain. He could have gripped the fleshy wrist and removed the hand from his lap, he could have yelled for her to stop, or at least stood up and moved to another seat, but in the end he had done nothing because when he looked up she was smiling at him, her teasing eyes saying that she knew all about his secret, and that he was as sinful in this little game of theirs as she was.

Mr Chang shifted in the chair. The phantom limb of a youthful swelling from half a century ago and the wetness afterwards made him unable to breathe in the twilight. He had never told his wife about the incident; she had not been the kind of woman who would make a man relive a humiliating memory like that.

She did not mean to embarrass him in any way, Meilan said; only she was curious why he had not thought of dancing with her. Mr Chang shook his head. Some people were destined to be friends, he said, and others strangers.

A man could break a woman's heart with that reply, and Meilan had to tell herself that she was lucky that she had not had a heart for all her adult life.

Neither spoke for a moment, and when Mr Chang asked if Meilan needed another cup of tea, she knew that her time was running out. 'Do you still play music?' she asked, eagerly grabbing the first topic that occurred to her.

'The one who understands the music has ridden the wings of the crane to heaven,' he said.

She thought of telling him how she had listened to the music coming from his unit years ago, through open windows in the summer evenings, behind piled coal outside his unit on winter nights. But a love story told forty years too late could only be a joke. Instead, she asked him about the strange instrument she had never seen. She might as well solve one mystery if this turned out to be her only chance to talk to him.

He looked at her as if surprised by her memory, and without a word withdrew from the living room. A moment later, he came back with a round-bellied instrument. He plucked the strings and shook his head at the off-tune. 'My father-in-law brought it from America but neither he nor my wife knew how to play it,' he said. 'It's a banjo.'

'Where did you learn to play it then?'

'I figured out myself. It was not that hard. My wife used to boast to her friends that I was the only banjo player in Beijing.'

'Was that true?' Meilan asked, watching him smile dreamily, remembering an old joke perhaps between husband and wife.

'I've not met another one in my life.'

'Am I not a lucky one to meet the only banjo player in this city, Uncle Fatty?'

Mr Chang nodded, trying to recover some old tunes. Meilan stood up and swung slowly to the music. In the soft twilight her face looked beautiful in a strange way that reminded him of his wife, but the woman, with her blind cheerfulness and loud voice, would not feel in his music what his wife had once felt. Perhaps this was what his wife had wanted for him, a woman who understood little, an antidote to death and loneliness.

'I have a great idea,' Meilan said when the music stopped. It took forty years for him to play banjo for her once, and neither of them had forty more years to waste. 'We should move into one unit and sell the other.'

'Why?' he asked, aware that he had not behaved as shocked or offended as he should have. If he told the story of the train ride to the woman in front of him would she laugh at him? Or perhaps she would tell an equally unseemly story, a joke that would crack them up like a pair of shameless oldsters at the Twilight Club.

'Garden Road is hot now, and we'll make good money.'

'What are we if the police come to check our household-register cards?'

'Neighbours, room-mates, cohabitants,' Meilan said. 'How much space does one need at our age?'

Indeed, he thought. In the semi-darkness he plucked the strings again. Sooner or later one of them would have to stand up and turn on the lamp, but for now he would like to think of himself as happily occupied, playing an old song on an older banjo.

JUNO MCKITTRICK

Bella

IT'S ALWAYS shadowy, that corner of the living room on July Street, unless I focus and see Pop lying on the table, one purple hand sticking out from under the white sheet. Which is daft, because I never saw him there at all. It was Bella who told me and he wasn't her pop anyway. He was just a big, old, tired pop her mother (the old harridan) found drowning the sorrows of widowerhood in the Neptune. Once, when we were eight, Bella asked her (the old barnacle) and she just said, 'Oh, that one? He always slept with a knife under his pillow . . .' Not whether he was dead or mad or in prison. I know he must have been handsome because 'You're pretty,' my sister once told me, 'but Bella's beautiful,' and it's true, she was, whereas her mother had a face like the back of a bus, as my mum used to say, with the skin like raw pastry and a slit of a mouth the colour of cochineal which my sister also said was got from crushing insects. She had a hump not even the moth-eaten fur coat could hide but her eyes were the worst. They never smiled, ever. Although we heard the uncles making her laugh sometimes. The uncles . . . those string-vested sailors who dumped their sea bags in the hall and hove to at the fag-ashed hearth.

Which was fine by us because the kitchen and garden were our domain. One of the uncles gave Bella a tent and as we drove the pegs in I wondered, seeing as the ground beneath us was no use to anyone else, did all of it, right through to the centre of the earth, millions of miles of it, belong to Bella and her mother and Pop and me, by association? At home Dad planted the parrot's sunflower seeds in an old brown sink and every summer they grew tall enough to turn their heads away from us and gaze over our backyard wall at the passers-by on the bomb-site. The bomb-site had groundsel and fireweed and blasted bricks growing there and a round stone wall protecting the Vicar and his daughters with little blue doors sinking into the ground at intervals and my sister said they must lead to the real secret garden and when there was no one about me and Bella used to go and stand under the overhanging trees and read aloud to each other from a small grey poem book I'd found in our cubbyhole. Poems by people whose names meant little to us, except, it seems to me, as part of a vague remembered dream: Rose Fyleman, Christina Rossetti, Walter de la Mare, adamantine names home from the silent land to tell us about 'the cool syringa's scented shade' and 'the bleak midwinter', which wasn't long ago and far away but began and ended here in the summer night with one or two sparrows calling and rubble melting into the dark and lights flashing on in the terraces where men sang in sculleries as they washed at little brown sinks and, often, poorly children perched by the black grates, watching hour by hour the coal shift and fall.

To sleep in Bella's tent I had to creep out of bed at midnight, sprint down our road and then turn right into July Street past cats sitting hopefully on doorsteps and dogs barking through letter boxes and one time, as we lay there with Buddy Holly telling us to 'rave on' from under the rough, grey blankets we heard also the man with two wives punching one of them in the alley. Bella said it didn't make sense because Rita was the one he liked best. When everyone had gone back in we crept out to look for the body and found none, although there were plenty on the stairs and in the hall where men wore their sagging flesh like ceremonial robes and time-honoured needs manifested themselves day or night.

How could a house so new feel so melancholy? I wondered.

I think Pop must have realised how stupid he'd been when he saw her (the old albatross) putting on the aforementioned fur thing without a glance at him, without a word to him, leaving him alone with his cough and forgetting the Guinness he'd hoped for.

The house always smelled of onions and often there was congealed gravy on the plates piled high in the sink, which occasionally I'd offer to dry as Bella washed. There were tea rings on the radiogram and thick dust lay everywhere. Bella did her best, but, like me, she had other commitments, such as school or playing out, and the house, so full of ghosts, resembled one of those beaten women who keeps her best, most treasured wedding photo on the dresser, fooling no one.

Still, things happened there that could never have happened at our house, like me being kissed by one of a gang of fly-by boys when I went to fetch the coal and to this day I can feel that kiss on my mouth. When I came to I was standing on the back step with the shovel in my hand and the air on fire and Bella shouting at me to hurry up with the coal as 'Marmee' would be back soon. Bella had been reading *Little Women* in her box of a bedroom which caught the late sun but held too a sort of sad transience and where, one evening (and I'll never remember why), we crept into her narrow bed in our vests and bottle-green gym knickers to lie all night with our arms tight around each other.

More than anything I want to ask her about what happened on Patmos Street. We never saw anyone there, either in the morning as we ran that way to school, or in the afternoon, drifting lazily home, or on Thursday after tea as I crept to my piano lesson and the big stick in the cupboard and the fierce dog rootling and snorting in the kitchen I could hear during the long silences I should have been filling with 'Blumenlied' or 'Blazeaway' – never saw anyone either leaning on a lamp post or scrubbing a step or so much as disturbing with their breath a single lace curtain and when the 'thing' happened it was midday and hot and there was neither footfall nor shadow along the whole length of the Edwardian terrace and Bella told me to go and listen at the door of number 44, the one with the name 'Cameron' on a tarnished plaque on the wall, tired green curtains going to grey, a sad aspidistra and no movement in the patches of sun that patterned the dust inside the still bay.

'All right,' I said, 'but don't go away,' trying to put my ear to the rusty keyhole and keep an eye on her at the same time. At first there was nothing. Nothing at all. Then, from far away, perhaps as far as a distant scullery where a dripping of water washed something clean in a sink, year in, year out the same cracked plate, or the pitch blackness of a cubbyhole under rotting stairs, came the little sad sounds of harp notes, playing for no one, unless for us on our way home from school, with nobody waiting to ask and nothing better to do than stand here and eavesdrop in the grime of our mutual absurdity and so small they were that I have never been sure they weren't simply the fulfilment of Bella's wish for me.

When I went to grammar school without her I started to get funny about things like my uniform. I made elaborate shows of inspecting her kitchen for grease before putting down my new blazer. I stopped offering to help with the washing up. The truth was I was out of my depth and could barely cope but Bella supposed I was clever and she believed I was happy.

So, little by little, I left her and the old tent and the voices in the alley and the dirty dishes and crates of empties and a dozen or so long-lost uncles and the fur thing on the banister and the ghosts on the stairs and the mystery of Patmos Street, all of which I like to think she used as stepping-stones because I heard she walked free one day.

I wish I had been there then. I wish I had seen her and cheered her on. I wonder about it, though. And her. I wonder about her all the time. And I'd like her to know that I'm cheering now.

LIZ DAY

Waving at the Gardener

MY GRANDCHILDREN don't like hand-knitted clothes any more, so I knit for the children in Russia. It's better really, I can knit smaller things, easier for me since I had my stroke. You see my left hand is very weak, although it is improving. Well, I think it is.

I sleep in the spare room now. Edward, that's my husband, moved me in here when I came out of hospital. I don't know why. He said I'd be more comfortable, but I miss my big bed.

Anyway, as I haven't been able to speak since my stroke I couldn't argue. I say I can't speak, but I can say one word – 'No'. It seems strange that's the only word I can say because I've always been such a 'yes' woman. You know the sort, always ready to please. 'Yes, I'll do the teas for the WI, yes, I'll babysit, yes, I'll do the collection for Heart Disease.' Hated letting people down, you see. I think that's part of the reason I had a stroke, ran myself ragged trying to please other people. Always agreed with my husband too. Well, women of my generation did. It made life easier too, even though it used to make my blood boil sometimes the way Edward used to go on about black people and gays, or 'queers' as he called them. Anyway, now I can only say 'No', which I think is really funny, it makes me laugh out loud, uncontrollably sometimes. Edward doesn't like that. 'Stop it, Monica,' he says when I start. 'Stop it or you'll make yourself ill again!' But I can only say 'No', which makes me laugh more. In the end he just walks out of the room. Edward wanted me to go into a nursing home when I was discharged from hospital. He even made some enquiries, but then he found out how much it would cost so he changed his mind. He thought the government would pay for it all, silly old fool. But we've got savings, money my parents left us, and he's got an excellent pension so the government certainly wasn't going to fork out. Social Services set up this 'care package', as they call it.

I have two carers, one to get me up in the morning and one to put me to bed. See, apart from losing the ability to speak I lost the use all down my left side, completely to begin with. I recovered quite a bit, but I can't really walk unaided and I tend to lose my balance sometimes. Of course Edward has to pay towards this 'care package'. I can tell that doesn't please him and he also has to pay someone to help with the housework too, and the gardening. My daughter-in-law Jenny says it's made him realise how much I used to do and I suppose it has.

Anyway, I'm quite happy in my little room. I listen to Radio 4 a lot and sometimes watch TV and of course I knit; that makes me feel I'm not totally useless. My friend Margaret brings me wool every now and then and sews things up when I've finished them. She also brings me magazines and books, and although Edward has told her I can't read any more she doesn't seem to be able to take that on board and still keeps bringing them. But I'm always glad to see her and she keeps me up to date with all the gossip.

Edward brings me a cup of tea in the morning at about seven and takes me to the toilet. I know he's terrified I'll wet the bed, but I never have. That kind of thing embarrasses him, you see, always has. While I'm enthroned in the bathroom I know he goes and checks the bed to see that it's dry, which makes me smile. Anyway, I manage to clean my teeth and then he helps me back to bed and switches on my radio.

He brings me my breakfast at eight, and then I wait for my carer. She's meant to come at nine o'clock, but she's so busy she often doesn't get to me until ten.

I've got two carers, Brenda and Pauline. They're both nice, hardworking girls and what I look forward to is the fact that they talk to me even though I can't answer. I hear all about their lives. Brenda has five children. The eldest, a boy, is always in trouble with the police and she doesn't know what to do with him. Apparently her husband is no help, always out fishing when he's not working. I'd like to say, 'Well, at least he's working,' you know, comfort her a bit, but of course I can't say anything. I just squeeze her hand and then she gives me a hug and says, 'I don't know what I'd do without you, Mrs P.' I suppose in a way it's good for her to be able to unload some of her worries on to me and I don't mind. Pauline's got her troubles too. She's a single mother, has three girls and the youngest has Down's syndrome. They used to call it mongolism in my day.

'My husband couldn't take it,' she told me one day. ' "It makes me feel ashamed," he said and then left, moved back in with his mother.' I wanted to say he should be more ashamed of moving back with his mother than having a disabled daughter, but of course I couldn't. Anyway, Pauline taught me to put my thumbs up when I want to say yes. I don't know why they didn't think of that at the hospital: too busy, I suppose.

Brenda or Pauline get me up, wash and dress me and take me downstairs. I do get a bit depressed about my clothes. When I was first ill, Jenny bought me three velvet-type tracksuits. I can see why: they were easier for everyone who was looking after me to cope with. But they were the last thing on earth I would have chosen to wear and now I'm slightly more mobile I long to wear some of my old clothes again. I'd always kept myself so smart before. One day, I dragged Brenda to the wardrobe in my old room and pointed to my other clothes. Of course all the time I was pointing I was saying, 'No, no, no,' but luckily she understood and we tried on one of my old skirts. Of course, it didn't fit. I'd lost so much weight. I cried then. Brenda was very kind and hugged me and said she'd talk to Jenny about my clothes. Jenny looks after my clothes, you see, and arranges for me to have my hair done once a week. She's a good girl.

After I'm downstairs, Edward brings me a cup of coffee. Well, I say cup, but actually he puts it in one of those plastic-beaker things with a spout. It makes the coffee taste awful and it's so unnecessary because I can hold a cup or mug quite well now, but of course I can't tell him that.

Edward doesn't sit with me. Sometimes he'll stand awkwardly by the window and say something like, 'Looks quite nice now,' or, 'The roses are good this year,' to which I invariably answer, 'No.' Then he makes some excuse and goes to work in his study or his shed and leaves me watching TV. It's funny this 'no' word. I can feel my brain searching around for the right words to use. It's as if they're all in a heap in my head instead of in neat rows. I find the word I want to say, but then 'no' comes out. It's really strange, and if I get really desperate to say something and try hard, 'No' comes out in triplicate, rather like that chap on *The Vicar of Dibley*, but sadly there's no 'yes' at the end.

When I first came out of hospital, the Vicar came to see me. Before I was ill I was a regular churchgoer; I used to do the flowers, polish brasses, you know, all the things that middle-class women do. Anyway, the Vicar came and sat with me, said a little prayer and told me how much everyone missed me. Edward, who isn't a regular attender, made him a cup of tea and then left us to it. Poor Vicar, he couldn't really cope, kept asking me questions. How did I feel? Did I think I was improving? How was hospital? Of course, I couldn't answer and then he said would I like someone to collect me and take me to communion once a month. I would have loved to go and became really excited, but I could only say, 'No, no, no,' even though I wanted to say, 'Yes.' I didn't think of putting my thumb up and the Vicar was so shocked he left soon after, didn't even drink his tea. I suppose he thought I'd lost my faith. I cried with frustration when he'd gone. I wanted to go to church so much but I couldn't tell anyone. Then I remembered the shocked look on the Vicar's face and began to laugh. Edward got worried; he's always worried if I act a bit strangely and of course I couldn't tell him what I was laughing at.

At one o'clock Edward gives me lunch. It's never anything very exciting, but he always cuts it up for me and ties a large serviette round my neck so I don't splash my clothes. I know he resents having to do the cooking and washing up and of course the shopping as well. Once, when he burnt something, he smashed the plate on the floor and stormed out of the house swearing. Just left me sitting at the table. Luckily Margaret called in and cleared everything up and gave me some soup. Poor Edward, I've wrecked his retirement really.

After lunch, I have a drink of water and Edward helps me back upstairs (we've got one of the stairlifts), takes me to the bathroom, of course, and then puts me to bed for a rest. I don't mind, I get quite tired and I like to listen to the afternoon play on the radio.

Sometimes at about four my two granddaughters Sarah and Jessica call in on their way home from school. They're fourteen, twins, and they light up my life. They don't mind that I can't talk; they just fill the room with chatter and laughter. I can't stop looking at them, with their long hair and beautiful eyes. I love them so much and it makes me want to cry because I can't tell them. I don't cry, of course; that might put them off coming or frighten them. I just smile at them and laugh with them. Usually they paint my nails for me and comb my hair. Once they made up my face. It was a bit garish, especially the gold eye shadow, but we had such fun. When they had gone Edward said to me, 'I'll be grateful when Brenda gets that muck off your face.'

At five o'clock Edward gets me into a chair by the window and brings me my tea. He's good at tea and it's the meal I enjoy most. I think it's because I can eat it on my own without Edward's disapproving looks if I drop crumbs or slurp my tea. It might be a poached egg on toast, that's my favourite, or beans on toast or cheese on toast. Some fruit or a piece of cake follows that, and a cup of tea. As I say, it's Edward's best meal and he's usually in quite a good mood. Probably because he's had the afternoon to himself.

About once a week my son Peter comes to see me. He's very comforting, sits on the bed and holds my hand. I want to tell him so many things but I can't. I can't even write it down, as my brain can't make sense of letters and words.

I just have my thoughts. He tells me about his work, and news of his son Jonathan, who's away at university. I don't know what I'd do without Peter and Jenny: they know what Edward is like.

At nine o'clock, one of my carers comes to put me to bed. This is particularly annoying if there's something I want to watch on television, but the girls are usually anxious to get home to their families so I don't make a fuss, not that I could really.

At about ten Edward comes up to bed. He comes to say goodnight and kisses me on the top of my head and then leaves me. I usually listen to the radio. If I can't sleep I often think about sex, which is really strange because I never used to before, before I was ill, I mean. Edward and I were never very active in that department even when we were younger and I used to wonder if I'd missed out at all. Well, now I know I have; you only have to watch TV to realise that, all that thrashing about and crying out. It was never like that with Edward and me, I can tell you. And why do I think about it now? Once when I was sitting downstairs I saw our gardener through the window. He's a young chap and he had taken his shirt off. He turned and smiled at me and gave me a little wave, and I suddenly realised I had missed something in my life, something wonderful although I wasn't sure what. But then that night I had the most amazing dream about him and all at once I knew. It made me sad, and angry with Edward, which is a bit unfair, I suppose, but men should know about these things. I can't help wondering why I am plagued with these thoughts now.

Something amazing happened the other day, well, it was a momentous day all round. When Edward brought my breakfast he was holding a letter. 'We've had a letter from the Stroke Association, Monica. They've got a place for you in the local dysphasia group.' He looked at me, his eyes shining. 'Isn't that grand? They will pick you up on Wednesday mornings, take you there, give you lunch and tea and bring you back about four.' He looked at me expectantly.

Of course I knew why he was so excited: he would be without me for a whole day. A whole day free to himself. For a moment I forgot about his bad moods and surliness and felt quite sorry for him, stuck with an invalid. I smiled lopsidedly and put my thumbs up.

'That's really good news, Monica. They have speech therapists there, you know.' He folded the letter up. 'I think I'll go and telephone Jenny.'

To my surprise he bent down and kissed me, not on top of the head as he usually does, but on my cheek. And then the most amazing thing happened. As he stood up, I said, 'OK,' just like that; it popped out like a cork out of a bottle. We stared at each other for a moment and then I said it again, three times, 'OK, OK, OK.' And we both started to laugh.

'Well, old girl, that's a turn up for the books. The doctor told me there was a chance you'd get some speech back.'

After he'd gone downstairs I said the word over and over. I suppose I was frightened it would go away again. The strange thing was, 'OK' isn't a word I would have used normally. After all, it's a slang word, isn't it?

They say good things come in threes, don't they? Whoever 'they' are. Well, after lunch, Jenny called round with a large carrier bag. 'I've been shopping, Mum, and bought you a couple of skirts, thought you could do with a change.'

Jenny, bless her, often talks to me as if I'm deaf or a bit of a halfwit, but she means well and is always very kind to me.

She held up two very attractive tweed skirts, just the sort of thing I would have chosen myself. I was so thrilled my eyes filled with tears and I grasped Jenny's hand so she wouldn't think I was sad. Then I remembered I could say 'OK', so I did, over and over again. We did laugh.

'I thought tights might me a bit difficult so I thought we'd try these hold-ups.' She held up a pair of stockings with lacy elasticated tops. They were beautiful and I began to laugh again. Of course they were the sort of thing that Edward would disapprove of, but it didn't matter now. Jenny had bought them.

Although it was afternoon, Edward had forgotten to take me back to bed and when Jenny had gone I sat in the sitting room looking out at our garden, which looked so pretty. And there, completing the picture for me, was our beautiful young gardener. He hadn't taken his top off this time, but I could still see his lovely young body working away under his T-shirt and jeans. He saw me watching and, bless him, smiled and gave me a wave. I grinned foolishly and lopsidedly and then waved back. A picture of those silky lacy stockings flashed into my head and I couldn't help laughing to myself. 'OK,' I said as I waved. 'OK, OK, OK.'

MARGARET ATWOOD

Rape Fantasies

THE WAY they're going on about it in the magazines you'd think it was just invented, and not only that but it's something terrific, like a vaccine for cancer. They put it in capital letters on the front cover, and inside they have these questionnaires like the ones they used to have about whether you were a good enough wife or an endomorph or an ectomorph, remember that? with the scoring upside down on page 73, and then these numbered do-it-yourself dealies, you know? 'RAPE, TEN THINGS TO DO ABOUT IT', like it was ten new hairdos or something. I mean, what's so new about it?

So at work they all have to talk about it because no matter what magazine you open there it is, staring you right between the eyes, and they're beginning to have it on the television, too. Personally I'd prefer a June Allyson movie any time but they don't make them any more and they don't even have them that much on the *Late Show*. For instance, day before yesterday, that would be Wednesday, thank God it's Friday as they say, we were sitting around in the women's lunch room – the *lunch* room, I mean you'd think you could get some peace and quiet in there – and Chrissy closes up the magazine she's been reading and says, 'How about it, girls, do you have rape fantasies?'

The four of us were having our game of bridge the way we always do, and I had a bare twelve points counting the singleton with not that much of a bid in anything. So I said one club, hoping Sondra would remember about the one-club convention, because the time before when I used that she thought I really meant clubs and she bid us up to three, and all I had was four little ones with nothing higher than a six, and we went down two and on top of that we were vulnerable. She is not the world's best bridge player. I mean, neither am I but there's a limit.

Darlene passed but the damage was done, Sondra's head went round like it was on ball bearings and she said, '*What* fantasies?'

'Rape fantasies,' Chrissy said. She's a receptionist and she looks like one; she's pretty but cool as a cucumber, like she's been painted all over with nail polish, if you know what I mean. Varnished. 'It says here all women have rape fantasies.'

'For Chrissake, I'm eating an egg sandwich,' I said, 'and I bid one club and Darlene passed.'

'You mean, like some guy jumping you in an alley or something,' Sondra said. She was eating her lunch, we all eat our lunches during the game, and she bit into a piece of that celery she always brings and started to chew away on it with this thoughtful expression in her eyes and I knew we might as well pack it in as far as the game was concerned.

'Yeah, sort of like that,' Chrissy said. She was blushing a little, you could see it even under her make-up.

'I don't think you should go out alone at night,' Darlene said. 'You put yourself in a position.' And I may have been mistaken but she was looking at me. She's the oldest, she's forty-one though you wouldn't know it and neither does she, but I looked it up in the employees' file. I like to guess a person's age and then look it up to see if I'm right; I let myself have an extra pack of cigarettes if I am, though I'm trying to cut down. I figure it's harmless as long as you don't tell. I mean, not everyone has access to that file, it's more or less confidential. But it's all right if I tell you, I don't expect you'll ever meet her, though you never know, it's a small world. Anyway.

'For *heaven*'s sake, it's only *Toronto*,' Greta said. She worked in Detroit for three years and she never lets you forget it, it's like she thinks she's a war hero or something, we should all admire her just for the fact that she's still walking this earth, though she was really living in Windsor the whole time, she just worked in Detroit. Which for me doesn't really count. It's where you sleep, right?

'Well, do you?' Chrissy said. She was obviously trying to tell us about hers but she wasn't about to go first, she's cautious, that one.

'I certainly don't,' Darlene said, and she wrinkled up her nose, like this, and I had to laugh. 'I think it's disgusting.' She's divorced, I read that in the file too, she never talks about it. It must've been years ago anyway. She got up and went over to the coffee machine and turned her back on us as though she wasn't going to have anything more to do with it.

'Well,' Greta said. I could see it was going to be between her and Chrissy. They're both blondes, I don't mean that in a bitchy way but they do try to outdress each other. Greta would like to get out of Filing, she'd like to be a receptionist too so she could meet more people. You don't meet much of anyone in Filing except other people in Filing. Me, I don't mind it so much, I have outside interests.

'Well,' Greta said, 'I sometimes think about, you know my apartment? It's got this little balcony, I like to sit out there in the summer and I have a few plants out there. I never bother that much about locking the door to the balcony, it's one of those sliding-glass ones, I'm on the eighteenth floor for heaven's sake, I've got a good view of the lake and the CN Tower and all. But I'm sitting around one night in my housecoat, watching TV with my shoes off, you know how you do, and I see this guy's feet, coming down past the window, and the next thing you know he's standing on the balcony, he's let himself down by a rope with a hook on the end of it from the floor above, that's the nineteenth, and before I can even get up off the chesterfield he's inside the apartment. He's all dressed in black with black gloves on' – I knew right away what show she got the black gloves off because I saw the same one – 'and then he, well, you know.'

'You know what?' Chrissy said, but Greta said, 'And afterwards he tells me that he goes all over the outside of the apartment building like that, from one floor to another, with his rope and hook . . . and then he goes out to the balcony and tosses his rope, and he climbs up it and disappears.'

'Just like Tarzan,' I said, but nobody laughed.

'Is that all?' Chrissy said. 'Don't you ever think about, well, I think about being in the bathtub, with no clothes on . . .'

'So who takes a bath in their clothes?' I said, you have to admit it's stupid when you come to think of it, but she just went on.

'. . . with lots of bubbles, what I use is Vitabath, it's more expensive but it's so relaxing, and my hair pinned up, and the door opens and this fellow's standing there . . .'

'How'd he get in?' Greta said.

'Oh, I don't know, through a window or something. Well, I can't very well get out of the bathtub, the bathroom's too small, and besides he's blocking the doorway, so I just *lie* there, and he starts to very slowly take his own clothes off, and then he gets into the bathtub with me.'

'Don't you scream or anything?' said Darlene. She'd come back with her cup of coffee, she was getting really interested. 'I'd scream like bloody murder.'

'Who'd hear me?' Chrissy said. 'Besides, all the articles say it's better not to resist, that way you don't get hurt.'

'Anyway, you might get bubbles up your nose,' I said, 'from the deep breathing,' and I swear all four of them looked at me like I was in bad taste, like I'd insulted the Virgin Mary or something. I mean, I don't see what's wrong with a little joke now and then. Life's too short, right?

'Listen,' I said, 'those aren't *rape* fantasies. I mean you aren't getting *raped*, it's just some guy you haven't met formally who happens to be more attractive than Derek Cummins' – he's the Assistant Manager, he wears elevator shoes or at any rate they have these thick soles and he has this funny way of talking, we call him Derek Duck – 'and you have a good time. Rape is when they've got a knife or something and you don't want to.'

'So what about you, Estelle,' Chrissy said. She was miffed because I laughed at her fantasy, she thought I was putting her down. Sondra was miffed too, by this time she'd finished her celery and she wanted to tell about hers, but she hadn't got in fast enough.

'All right, let me tell you one,' I said. 'I'm walking down this dark street at night and this fellow comes up and grabs my arm. Now it so happens that I have a plastic lemon in my purse, you know how it always says you should carry a plastic lemon in your purse? I don't really do it, I tried it once but the darn thing leaked all over my chequebook, but in this fantasy I have one, and I say to him, "You're intending to rape me, right?" and he nods, so I open my purse to get the plastic lemon, and I can't find it! My purse is full of all this junk, Kleenex and cigarettes and my change purse and my lipstick and my driver's licence, you know the kind of stuff; so I ask him to hold out his hands, like this, and I pile all this junk into them and down at the bottom there's the plastic lemon, and I can't get the top off. So I hand it to him and he's very obliging, he twists the top off and hands it back to me, and I squirt him in the eye.'

I hope you don't think that's too vicious. Come to think of it, it is a bit mean, especially when he was so polite and all.

'*That's* your rape fantasy?' Chrissy says. 'I don't believe it.'

'She's a card,' Darlene says. She and I are the ones that've been here the longest and she never will forget the time I got drunk at the office party and insisted I was going to dance under the table instead of on top of it. I did a sort of Cossack number but then I hit my head on the bottom of the table – actually it was a desk – when I went to get up, and I knocked myself out cold. She's decided that's the mark of an original mind and she tells everyone new about it and I'm not sure that's fair. Though I did do it.

'I'm being totally honest,' I say. I always am and they know it. There's no point in being anything else is the way I look at it, and sooner or later the truth will out so you might as well not waste the time, right? 'You should hear the one about the Easy-Off oven cleaner.'

But that was the end of the lunch hour, with one bridge game shot to hell, and the next day we spent most of the time arguing over whether to start a new game or play out the hands we had left over from the day before, so Sondra never did get a chance to tell about her rape fantasy.

It started me thinking, though, about my own rape fantasies. Maybe I'm abnormal or something, I mean I have fantasies about handsome strangers coming in through the window too, like Mr Clean, I wish one would, please God somebody without flat feet and big sweat marks on his shirt, and over five feet five, believe me being tall is a handicap though it's getting better, tall guys are starting to like someone whose nose reaches higher than their belly button. But if you're being totally honest you can't count those as rape fantasies. In a real rape fantasy, what you should feel is this anxiety, like when you think about your apartment building catching on fire and whether you should use the elevator or the stairs or maybe just stick your head under a wet towel and you try to remember everything you've read about what to do but you can't decide.

For instance, I'm walking along this dark street at night and this short, ugly fellow comes up and grabs my arm, and not only is he ugly, you know, with a sort of puffy nothing face, like those fellows you have to talk to in the bank when your account's overdrawn – of course I don't mean they're all like that – but he's absolutely covered in pimples. So he gets me pinned against the wall, he's short but he's heavy, and he starts to undo himself and the zipper gets stuck. I mean, one of the most significant moments in a girl's life, it's almost like getting married or having a baby or something, and he sticks the zipper.

So I say, kind of disgusted, 'Oh for Chrissake,' and he starts to cry. He tells me he's never been able to get anything right in his entire life, and this is the last straw, he's going to go jump off a bridge.

'Look,' I say, I feel so sorry for him, in my rape fantasies I always end up feeling sorry for the guy, I mean there has to be something *wrong* with them; if it was Clint Eastwood it'd be different but worse luck it never is. I was the kind of little girl who buried dead robins, know what I mean? It used to drive my mother nuts, she didn't like me touching them, because of the germs, I guess. So I say, 'Listen, I know how you feel. You really should do something about those pimples. If you got rid of them you'd be quite good-looking, honest; then you wouldn't have to go around doing stuff like this. I had them myself once,' I say, to comfort him, but in fact I did, and it ends up I give him the name of my old dermatologist, the one I had in high school, that was back in Leamington, except I used to go to St Catharine's for the dermatologist. I'm telling you, I was really lonely when I first came here; I thought it was going to be such a big adventure and all, but it's a lot harder to meet people in a city. But I guess it's different for a guy.

Or I'm lying in bed with this terrible cold, my face is all swollen up, my eyes are red and my nose is dripping like a leaky tap, and this fellow comes in through the window and *he* has a terrible cold too, it's a new kind of flu that's been going around. So he says, 'I'b goig do rabe you' – I hope you don't mind me holding my nose like this but that's the way I imagine it – and he lets out this terrific sneeze, which slows him down a bit, also I'm no object of beauty myself, you'd have to be some kind of pervert to want to rape someone with a cold like mine, it'd be like raping a bottle of LePages mucilage the way my nose is running.

He's looking wildly around the room, and I realise it's because he doesn't have a piece of Kleenex! 'Id's ride here,' I say, and I pass him the Kleenex, God knows why he even bothered to get out of bed; you'd think if you were going to go around climbing in windows you'd wait till you were healthier, right? I mean, that takes a certain amount of energy. So I ask him why doesn't he let me fix him a NeoCitran and Scotch, that's what I always take, you still have the cold but you don't feel it, so I do and we end up watching the *Late Show* together. I mean, they aren't all sex maniacs, the rest of the time they must lead a normal life. I figure they enjoy watching the *Late Show* just like anybody else.

I do have a scarier one, though, where the fellow says he's hearing angel voices that're telling him he's got to kill me, you know, you read about things like that all the time in the papers. In this one I'm not in the apartment where I live now, I'm back in my mother's house in Leamington and the fellow's been hiding in the cellar. He grabs my arm when I go downstairs to get a jar of jam and he's got hold of the axe too, out of the garage, that one is really scary. I mean, what do you say to a nut like that?

So I start to shake but after a minute I get control of myself and I say is he sure the angel voices have got the right person, because I hear the same angel voices and they've been telling me for some time that I'm going to give birth to the reincarnation of St Anne who in turn has the Virgin Mary and right after that comes Jesus Christ and the end of the world, and he wouldn't want to interfere with that, would he? So he gets confused and listens some more, and then he asks for a sign and I show him my vaccination mark, you can see it's sort of an odd-shaped one, it got infected because I scratched the top off, and that does it, he apologises and climbs out the coal chute again, which is how he got in in the first place, and I say to myself there's some advantage in having been brought up a Catholic even though I haven't been to church since they changed the service into English, it just isn't the same, you might as well be a Protestant. I must write to Mother and tell her to nail up that coal chute, it always has bothered me. Funny, I couldn't tell you at all what this man looks like but I know exactly what kind of shoes he's wearing, because that's the last I see of him, his shoes going up the coal chute, and they're the old-fashioned kind that lace up the ankles, even though he's a young fellow. That's strange, isn't it?

Let me tell you though I really sweat until I see him safely out of there and I go upstairs right away and make myself a cup of tea. I don't think about that one much. My mother always said you shouldn't dwell on unpleasant things and I generally agree with that, I mean dwelling on them doesn't make them go away. Though not dwelling on them doesn't make them go away either when you come to think of it.

Sometimes I have these short ones where the fellow grabs my arm but I'm really a kung fu expert, can you believe it; in real life I'm sure it would just be a conk on the head and that's that, like getting your tonsils out, you'd wake up and it would be all over except for the sore places, and you'd be lucky if your neck wasn't broken or something; I could never even hit the volleyball in gym and a volleyball is fairly large, you know? – and I just go *zap* with my fingers into his eyes and that's it, he falls over, or I flip him against a wall or something. But I could never really stick my fingers in anyone's eyes, could you? It would feel like hot jello and I don't even like cold jello, just thinking about it gives me the creeps. I feel a bit guilty about that one, I mean how would you like walking around knowing someone's been blinded for life because of you?

But maybe it's different for a guy.

The most touching one I have is when the fellow grabs my arm and I say, sad and kind of dignified, 'You'd be raping a corpse.' That pulls him up short and I explain that I've just found out I have leukaemia and the doctors have only given me a few months to live. That's why I'm out pacing the streets alone at night, I need to think, you know, come to terms with myself. I don't really have leukaemia but in the fantasy I do. I guess I chose that particular disease because a girl in my grade-four class died of it, the whole class sent her flowers when she was in the hospital. I didn't understand then that she was going to die and I wanted to have leukaemia too so I could get flowers. Kids are funny, aren't they? Well, it turns out that he has leukaemia himself, and *he* only has a few months to live, that's why he's going around raping people, he's very bitter because he's so young and his life is being taken from him before he's really lived it. So we walk along gently under the street lights, it's spring and sort of misty, and we end up going for coffee, we're happy we've found the only other person in the world who can understand what we're going through, it's almost like fate, and after a while we just sort of look at each other and our hands touch, and he comes back with me and moves into my apartment and we spend our last months together before we die, we just sort of don't wake up in the morning, though I've never decided which one of us gets to die first. If it's him I have to go and fantasise about the funeral, if it's me I don't have to worry about that, so it just about depends on how tired I am at the time. You may not believe this but sometimes I even start crying. I cry at the ends of movies, even the ones that aren't all that sad, so I guess it's the same thing. My mother's like that too.

The funny thing about these fantasies is that the man is always someone I don't know, and the statistics in the magazines, well, most of them anyway, they say it's often someone you do know, at least a little bit, like your boss or something – I mean, it wouldn't be *my* boss, he's over sixty and I'm sure he couldn't rape his way out of a paper bag, poor old thing, but it might be someone like Derek Duck, in his elevator shoes, perish the thought – or someone you just met, who invites you up for a drink, it's getting so you can hardly be sociable any more, and how are you supposed to meet people if you can't trust them even that basic amount? You can't spend your whole life in the Filing Department or cooped up in your own apartment with all the doors and windows locked and the shades down. I'm not what you would call a drinker but I like to go out now and then for a drink or two in a nice place, even if I am by myself. I'm with Women's Lib on that even though I can't agree with a lot of the other things they say. Like here, for instance, the waiters all know me and if anyone, you know, bothers me . . . I don't know why I'm telling you all this, except I think it helps you get to know a person, especially at first, hearing some of the things they think about. At work they call me the office worry wart, but it isn't so much like worrying, it's more like figuring out what you should do in an emergency, like I said before.

Anyway, another thing about it is that there's a lot of conversation, in fact I spend most of my time, in the fantasy, that is, wondering what I'm going to say and what he's going to say; I think it would be better if you could get a conversation going. Like, how could a fellow do that to a person he's just had a long conversation with? Once you let them know you're human, you have a life too, I don't see how they could go ahead with it, right? I mean, I know it happens but I just don't understand it, that's the part I really don't understand.

CATHERINE CHANTER

A Summary of Findings

D A DA diddle diddle da da. The grey body of her mobile
phone is cancan-ing on the table reminding her of the
rat squatting in her oven, rattling round unseen on the
grease-smeared tins, and the ratman says, 'It's better than
having a bun in the oven.'

'I wouldn't mind,' she replies.

And he says, 'Well, I'm one heck of a baker.'*

It's very close to the edge, she thinks, and she knows that if
she can only stand up she can stop the vibrating mobile from
toppling on to the floor, with the toast crusts and the ants and
the dirt from the dust and the debris. If she can only stand up.

There's no money for another if it breaks. But her Ryan
is a right little Oliver Twist despite all she's done, hanging
around and out at all hours, and there's guns and there's
gangs and there's men on the news who like little boys
in just the same way that they used to like her. Oh, he'll
nick one for her and then they'll be off again, on the same
old roundabout of police on the doorstep, probation on
the phone.† It's just like when the man on the waltzers at

---

* The Housing Association report that on a recent visit the property
was 'infested'. The PCO made suggestions to Ms M about the state of
affairs. (*See Appendix A*)

† Police records show that the R was issued with an ASBO due to TDA.
He was placed on the YOT waiting list for a diversionary project in
November.

Butlins comes up behind and spins you around, even if you're yelling that you want to get off and your dad says can't take you anywhere, look at the mess when you're sick on the steps.

The cancan finishes and there is a pause for the audience to burst into applause and the relief is so great that the absence of noise is as loud as the silence. Then other sounds from the flat creep possessively into the space between the right ear and the left, because they don't like a vacuum, the voices don't. The radio turns up the volume. The television grows jealous next door. The restless guests are heading for the screen. There they are in the corner of her mind's eye. With hitched skirts and crotchtight trousers, they lift their legs like pissing dogs to clamber out of the daytime chat show and into her front room: the even-fatter-than-her woman, the even-angrier-than-her son, the haranguing audience who rampage down the aisles and out through the TV until the room is full, piling into her head like mates at a party heading for the kitchen when the booze has run out in the hall.

Calli swallows the disturbance, past her lumping oesophagus, but one pill[*] isn't enough to prevent the outside noises who are now eager to break in. The sirens. The slamming doors. The f-ing this and f-ing that on the walkway. The languages she doesn't understand and why should she? It's enough to know that they are talking about her.

Da da dadldl da. This mobile is demanding. Calli is bemused, unsure that it is really hers – this miracle birth of modern technology. Dada. She could cradle it, caress it,

* Dr Price confirms that he issued Ms M with a repeat prescription for Nardil (MAOI phenelzine). He alerted her to the risk of combining MAOI family with alcohol and OTC remedies.

but it is never satisfied and she cannot understand why it never stops crying. Da. Why should she care for him when he gives nothing back to her?[*] When he doesn't come back to her. Like the daisy chains she made on the grassy bank by the holiday chalet when she was the same age as Ryan, she threads together the possibilities of who it might be. If it isn't the loans, it will be housing. If it isn't housing, it will be the surgery. If it isn't the surgery, it will be the unit. She can't remember what you do with the last daisy.

Da da dadldl da da. Most likely the unit.

Unit. You should have seen her mum knit. Unpicking the outgrown polo necks into yards of curlywurly wool and knitting them up again into patchwork blankets of many colours for the grandchildren. Do you remember this one, looking so lovely in it, that day at the beach with the wind in your hair and your hair in your eyes and the nits in your hair. She has bought a thin comb with mean teeth. She will never let him go through what she'd had to go through with the nits in her hair and the wind in her eyes and the tears on her cheeks in the one-day-to-be-unravelled jumper.

Who would have thought she'd have a kid who went to a unit? Hundreds, tens and units. He loved his maths at the old school, sitting in front of the telly with his black-and-blue scrapelegs tucked under him and the tables up to twelveses and the mobile on the table.[†]

She is sad that she wasn't able to help him then and she isn't able to help him now. Because of the units, Doctor Price says.

[*] Ms M was classified as high risk according to the EPDS, but PND support was withdrawn when she moved house.
[†] R. was p.ex from St John's for violent assault. He was placed at Action + for SEBD and sent to the PRU in February.

And drunk at the table at two in the morning, her friend Jen says, 'Oh all doctors ask how much you drink and if you look like us, with the ghosts of black eyes in the back of your head, they double the number.'

'So if I halve it and he doubles it, that's about right! Open another!'

'But you don't know your halveses, Calli, that's the problem. Shit! It's gone all over the floor!'

'The toast crusts have gone all pink!'

'And it's drowning the ants, poor buggers!'

'Just like the Red Sea . . .'

'You what?'

'The Red Sea. I saw a colour picture once, in one of those bibles they put in your chalet.'

And Jen says, 'You and your holiday villages . . .'*

One message received. The flab on Calli's arms hangs like fruit bats beneath her cave-grey T-shirt. Her breasts spread themselves flaccid and redundant on her stomach, like pale sunbathers on a convenient hump in the sand, and she is overwhelmed with the impossibility of lifting them all, these leaden, lethargic limbs, these ponderous parts of her, and carrying them to the table. The sweat from her spreading thighs seeps out from under her tight, short skirt and sticks her legs to the pink plastic seat. Maybe she will never get up.

If it wasn't for the fact that the lighter is on the counter, between her bag and the photo of her and her mum at her fiftieth – which was a laugh and a half and who would have known then what we know now that she'd never make it

* The Assertive Outreach Team referred Ms M to a project where support is available for alcohol abuse, addiction and obesity, but as she failed to attend two appointments in a row she forfeited her place on the programme.

to Christmas[*] – if it wasn't for that lighter, she wouldn't have got up and read the text. Like the tide at the seaside that summer, covering and uncovering the mudflats, Calli knows the calls must come in and go out, whether she likes it or not, and at this point she thinks nothing will ever change. Who would have thought she could have made a call, left the house, seen the balloon, made a plan. Who would have thought it.

'Tenford Pupil Referral Unit, how can I help?'

This is the secretary answering. She must have two jobs because Calli recognises her as the nice lady who says Harrow on the Hill on the Metropolitan line, as if she is reciting a nursery rhyme and putting all the passengers to bed. Calli would like to be tucked up by her and sleep for ever.

'It's Calli.'

'Thank you for calling back, Ms Mark. If you can just hold on and stand back behind the yellow line.'

Calli takes a step back so as not to be caught by the blast.

'Just putting you through to the Head.'

'Ms Mark. Thank you for calling back. Can you collect your son immediately from collection point A.'

(Because the Head is also the woman at Argos in charge of taking away.)[†]

Calli's unsteady hand drops the phone to the floor, where it spins on its head like a break-dancer amongst the bottle tops and cigarette ends and encircling applause on the steps

[*] The local Bereavement Counselling group did try to make contact following the unexpected death of Ms M's mother.
[†] The Headteacher referred R to Social Care. Following assessment, R & A concluded it was not necessary to instigate CP or Care Proceedings at that time.

of the leisure centre where she waits for the 52. The rain alone is constant. The tyres on the puddles and the lorries in the drizzle are the smells of the days when the bus never comes and empty beer cans and sodden newspapers bob on the belching drains, like the rubbish at the edge of the boating lake. But the glimpse of the sun in the patch of blue (big enough to patch a sailor's jacket, they'd said at the fiftieth) is the scent of a day when it's just around the corner and here it is.

The grey box next to the door of the unit is the fourth person she has spoken to that day. One times four is four. She must have said something to the girl who kneels by the news and prays by the papers on the floor of the newsagent's, but she cannot remember what. Mechanical words, they must have been, with nothing of her left in them at all. Words selected, picked up, swung over and dropped by a claw like the crane at the funfair, scooping and scraping, but always just missing the bear.[*]

While she is waiting for a reply, Calli watches a woman inching a buggy up the steep street towards her, looking for all the world as if the baby might win and send her back to the bottom again. Calli hears her breathless singing and sees a balloon tied to the handle, dancing in time to the song, as she crests the brow of the hill. Calli finds herself filling up with an idea until she feels she will burst into a million fragments which will float into the blue sky – enough to sew a galaxy of diamond sequins on the sailor's jacket. It is so obvious that she can't think why she never thought of it before. She will tie the red thread of a heart-shaped balloon round her wrist and sing and dance and win the talent show all over again, fluffing her rockabilly

[*] The shop assistant at the local newsagent who spoke to Ms M on the afternoon in question did not notice anything disturbing in her demeanour. (*See Appendix B*)

skirt and flinging her white knee-highs, with glimpses of green knickers for the men in the front row, stroking their beers with rough thumbs. Ryan will come with her: the two of them will cling tight on the waltzers and mock the man spinning them round, telling him faster, faster, see if we care; they will pedal a pink boat on the dark lake, their wake lifting the litter to the lapping edge; they will get the claws of the crane to rescue the bear and then celebrate with chips in the saltsea air – and a unit or two for her. A sort of lightness lifts Calli, inflated with the heady helium of the balloon. The door opens and the Head excludes her son back into her longing hands, back into their gangland arms. Look how beautiful he is, my son.

'The vicious nature of the assault means that we simply can't . . .'

'I've got a plan . . .'

'I'm pleased to hear that you are feeling positive about the future, but . . .'

'We're getting away from it all . . .'

'But if you're taking your son out of school then you'll need to notify . . .'

'You must know yourself what a difference it makes . . .'

'I know it's hard, Ms Mark, but you have to understand there's no miracle . . .'

'I went there myself and you should have seen us, my mum and my nan, wild they were on the big wheel, with Wales rising and falling over the Bristol Channel and me of all people winning the talent show! Say goodbye to your teacher, goodbye!'

Goodbye, Harrow on the Hill. We are back behind the yellow line.*

* The Headteacher said that Ms M seemed in a positive frame of mind, planning a holiday for herself and her son.

Ryan is out the door again and they've only been in a minute and no one knows then what we know now, that he'll never be back and the knife in his hand will be the death of him.[*] Calli sits down. She needs a fag and a unit or two to get over it all, but then she'll call Jen and tell her the plan. After the call, she'll do something about the floor because what would her mum say if she dropped round for tea and after the floor she'll see to their supper and after the supper they'll curl up on the sofa, his head on her shoulder, and for each hour he's not back she'll just have another, for hour after hour, just have another, to deal with the worry of being a mother and him being later and later and later . . .

The grey mobile squats on the kitchen table, quite close to the edge, offering an elbow to the chain of dancers or daisies in the wings, waiting to take or make the call. Dada diddle diddle dada.

Appendix A

– Number 58? Wasn't that the last rat job you did?
– What d'you do to her then? Overdose on the warfarin?
– Puts a new meaning on Rentokil, dunnit.
– Tell you, mate, if anyone OD'd, it was her. I felt sorry for her.
– Lonely, was she?
– Get in the van and give it a rest. Look at my face. I'm not laughing.

---

[*] The problem of gangs in the area has been well documented in 'Young, Wasted and White: a report into youth disaffection and drugs', HMSO 119C/31. (*See Appendix C*)

Appendix B

Although she was irritated by the dirty lino messing up her emerald-green salwar kameez, Salma knelt so she could stack the local papers neatly on the bottom shelf. Her business studies course had taught her the importance of display, that and the three Ps: product, price, politeness. On the front page of each of the one hundred and ten papers there was a picture of the woman and her son. Salma had never seen them together before, but she knew that the racist thug who lobbed stones at their window was the son of the fat woman who talked to herself and bought twenty B & H. She thought she should be forgiven for not having been polite to either of them. Since the police had been round, she had lurched between celebrity thrill and dry-mouthed guilt. Her mobile rang. It was Ibrar who had told her that people got what they deserved. She didn't feel she could talk to him about it, even if they were engaged.

Appendix C

U was my real friend and u left me here in this shit world. I luv u ryan and nothin going to stop that even now your mum waz nice to

Whitehill Mash Boyz aint goin to let this rest. RVENGE

RYAN U were to young to die. Live on in us whitehill mash boyz

Further appendices are available on request.

A Note on the Authors

MARGARET ATWOOD is the author of more than thirty books of fiction, poetry and critical essays. In addition to the classic *The Handmaid's Tale*, her novels include *Cat's Eye*, which was shortlisted for the Booker Prize, *Alias Grace*, which won the Giller Prize in Canada and the Premio Mondello in Italy, and *The Blind Assassin*, winner of the 2000 Booker Prize. *Oryx and Crake* was shortlisted for the Man Booker Prize in 2003. She was awarded the Prince of Asturias Prize for Literature in 2008. Her new novel *The Year of the Flood* is published in September 2009. She lives in Toronto, Canada.

CATHERINE CHANTER grew up in the West Country, studied English literature at Oxford and initially worked as a lobbyist in the UK and in the USA. Having become disillusioned with the political process, she returned to the UK in the early 1990s, retrained and has since worked in a wide range of settings with children with significant emotional and behavioural difficulties. This work has inspired much of her writing, as has the landscape in South Shropshire where she spends holidays. Catherine has written programmes for Radio 4 and has had poetry and short stories published in anthologies and journals including *Envoi, Leaf Books* and *Earlyworks Press*. Her short story 'The Boys' Guide to Winning: No. 1 Hide and Seek' was the runner up in the Bristol Short Story Prize 2008 and her novella *Rooms of the Mind* will be published by Cinnamon Press early next year.

JANNA CONNERTON was born in 1980 and grew up in East Sussex. She has a degree in politics and international studies from Warwick University and an MA in Middle East politics from Durham University. She is a qualified teacher and now works in a residential college for young adults with Asperger's syndrome. She attends a creative writing group in which she has been exploring the possibilities of the short story. She now lives in Frome, Somerset.

LIZ DAY has been a member of the Stort Valley Writers' Group for twenty years. She has had stories published in various magazines and has been runner-up in *Writers' News* and *Writing Magazine* short-story and poetry competitions. She says she can't remember a time when she was not writing something. Before taking early retirement she was a medical secretary working for the local health authority. Her favourite authors are Barbara Pym, E.F. Benson, Anita Brookner and Patrick Gale.

ALISON DUNN studied creative writing at the University of Sussex and enjoys writing poetry and fiction. Working in international development, she has spent several years in rural West Africa and is currently based in Brighton.

ALEXANDRA FOX lives in a small village in Northamptonshire. She is a mother, grandmother and freelance copy editor. Her short fiction has been published in magazines, anthologies and online. She has won numerous short-story competitions and was runner-up in Asham, Bridport and Fish prizes.

ESTHER FREUD's first novel, *Hideous Kinky*, was made into a feature film. She has published five subsequent novels, the most recent of which is *Love Falls*. Her stories have appeared in anthologies and magazines and she was named as one of the twenty Best of Young British Novelists by *Granta*.

VICKY GRUT's stories have appeared in literary magazines and collections, including *Random Factor* (Pulp Books 1997); *Valentine's Day: Stories of Revenge* (Duckworth 2000), two volumes of the British Council anthology *New Writing: 13* (Picador 2005) and *New Writing: 14* (Granta 2006). She was also a finalist in the 1999 Asham Award. She teaches creative writing for the Open University and at London's South Bank University.

YIYUN LI's stories and essays have been published in *The New Yorker*, *Best American Short Stories*, *The O. Henry Prize Stories*, and elsewhere. She has received grants and awards from Lannan Foundation and Whiting Foundation, and was named by *Granta* as one of the Best Young American Novelists. Her debut collection, *A Thousand Years of Good Prayers*, won the Frank O'Connor International Short Story Award, PEN/Hemingway Award, *Guardian* First Book Award, and California Book Award for first fiction. *A Thousand Years of Good Prayers*, the film adapted from the title story, recently won the Golden Shell for best film and a Silver Shell for best actor at San Sebastián International Film Festival in Spain. Her first novel *The Vagrants* was published in February 2009. Yiyun Li lives in Oakland, California with her husband and their two children.

JO LLOYD was brought up in Wales and now lives in Oxford. Her stories have been longlisted for the Bridport Prize and she has won this year's *Willesden Herald* Short Story Prize, for her story 'Work'.

ALISON MacLEOD grew up in Canada and moved to the UK in 1987 after accepting a place on the University of Lancaster's MA programme in creative writing. She published her first short story that year and her stories have since appeared in a variety of UK and Canadian magazines and collections. Her first novel, *The Changeling*, was published by Macmillan UK and St Martin's Press in 1996. Her second novel, *The Wave Theory of Angels*, was published by Hamish Hamilton and Penguin Canada in 1995. Her short-story collection, *Fifteen Modern Tales of Attraction*, was published by Penguin in 2007. She teaches on the MA programme in creative writing at the University of Chichester and lives in Brighton. More about her work can be found at *www.alison-macleod.com*.

JUNO McKITTRICK is in her sixties and was born in Walton, Liverpool. She started writing at the age of seven and has been writing (mainly poetry) ever since. She has recently started writing short stories seriously. She married a rock guitarist in the 1960s but has since divorced. She lives in Shropshire with her two daughters and works as a nursing assistant in a psychiatric unit.

NORA MORRISON is a Scot who has lived and worked in Jamaica, Wales, Cornwall and Malawi. Currently based in North Yorkshire, she makes frequent trips to Africa. She has an MA in English literature, a degree in psychology, has taught in schools and university and ran a head-hunting business for several years. Four years ago she was one of forty-eight writers shortlisted out of seventeen thousand in the BBC End of Story competition and was one of the final six who completed a story by Ian Rankin. She has just completed her first crime novel and is busy plotting her second.

HILARY PLEWS is the daughter of Irish Protestants who joined the British Army and she uses this heritage in her writing to explore identity. The experiences of working as a community lawyer with refugees and in carers' development are reflected in some of her short stories, one of which appeared in the Asham collection *Shoe Fly Baby*. She has completed the first draft of a novel.

ERICA ROCCA is a Lancastrian with Italian ancestry. She currently works as a TESOL teacher in the UK and plans to live and work in Europe. Her latest works include a play about the lives of women caught up in human trafficking and a series of short stories about the glory and sadness of love.

CHERISE SAYWELL grew up in Australia and has lived in the UK for over a decade. She won the V.S. Pritchett Prize in 2003 and has published her short stories in *The London Magazine*, *New Writing Scotland* and *Carve Magazine*. She recently finished writing her first novel (with the help of a Scottish Arts Council bursary), and is now working on her second. She lives in Edinburgh with her partner and their two young children.

A Note on the Type

The text of this book is set in Linotype Sabon, named
after the type founder, Jacques Sabon. It was designed
by Jan Tschichold and jointly developed by Linotype,
Monotype and Stempel, in response to a need for a
typeface to be available in identical form for
mechanical hot metal composition and
hand composition using foundry type.

Tschichold based his design for Sabon roman on a fount
engraved by Garamond, and Sabon italic on a fount by
Granjon. It was first used in 1966 and has proved an
enduring modern classic.